I Heard the Twang of Love and It Hurt My Ears

Edited by
Dean Wesley Smith

Stories from Pulphouse

FICTION MAGAZINE

I Heard the Twang of Love and It Hurt My Ears

Published by WMG Publishing Inc.
All stories reprinted from the pages of
Pulphouse Fiction Magazine
Cover and interior design copyright © 2024 WMG Publishing, Inc.
Cover art copyright © by fabioberti_it | Depositphotos

ISBN 13 (Trade Paperback): 978-1-56146-999-4

MORE FROM PULPHOUSE

MORE STORIES FROM *PULPHOUSE FICTION MAGAZINE*

A Twist of a Knife

Alibi Murder

Aliens Among Us

Cattitude Edited

Destination Tomorrow or Yesterday

Don't Touch My Magic!

Ghosts Among Us

History Repeats for No Reason

Implode the Membrane

Jingle My Bells

No Way: Totally Twisted Tales

Run!! Creatures, Critters, and Pulphousers…

Snot-Nosed Aliens

That's Really Messed Up

There'll Be Blue Popcorn Without You!

Three Sheets to the Wind

Twisted Robots, Oh, My!

STORIES FROM THE ORIGINAL PULPHOUSE

Stories from the Original Pulphouse: A Fiction Magazine

Stories from Pulphouse: The Hardback Magazine

GHOST OF A CHANCE

The Poker Chip: A Ghost of a Chance Novel

The Christmas Gift: A Ghost of a Chance Novel

The Free Meal: A Ghost of a Chance Novel

The Cop Car: A Ghost of a Chance Novella

The Deep Sunset: A Ghost of a Chance Novel

MARBLE GRANT

The First Year: A Marble Grant Novel

Time for Cool Madness: Six Crazy Marble Grant Stories

PAKHET JONES

The Big Tom: A Packet Jones Short Novel

Big Eyes: A Packet Jones Short Novel

THUNDER MOUNTAIN

Thunder Mountain

Monumental Summit

Avalanche Creek

The Edwards Mansion

Lake Roosevelt

Warm Springs

Melody Ridge

Grapevine Springs

The Idanha Hotel

The Taft Ranch

Tombstone Canyon

Dry Creek Crossing

Hot Springs Meadow

Green Valley

SEEDERS UNIVERSE

Dust and Kisses: A Seeders Universe Prequel Novel

Against Time

Sector Justice

Morning Song

The High Edge

Star Mist

Star Rain

Star Fall

Starburst

Rescue Two

CONTENTS

I Heard the Twang of Love and It Hurt My Ears

INTRODUCTION

DEAN WESLEY SMITH

I have no idea where I come up with these anthology titles. I think backers try to hit the stretch goals in the *Pulphouse Fiction Magazine* Kickstarter campaign just to see if I can actually come up with stories that fit the silly titles,

I know I worry about it when I go to doing these, usually about ten months after I came up with them.

But weirdly enough, this one is an easy one for me. You see, I love writing romance in a lot of my novels. Like everything I do, few of the books are straight romance. (Actually none of them are. They are science fiction, fantasy, or historical mixed with romance.)

But all of them have romance elements, so as an editor, I am drawn to romance elements in stories.

Take for example, Lisa Silverthorne's "A Game of Virgins." It is a wonderful send-up of the old trope of dragons and knights and so on. Not a real romance, but taking the idea of romance and really twisting it. I love that.

And Dayle A Dermatis's story "If the Shoe Fits" is a fantastically fun take on the entire Cinderella story, again taking romance and giving it a little flick on the nose.

So for both of those and other stories in this volume, my really silly title really does fit in more ways than one.

Hope you enjoy the read.

Dean Wesley Smith
Las Vegas, NV

LIVE THE PULPHOUSE LIFE!

Grab your Pulphouse mug and fill it with your favorite
beverage and lounge in your coziest chair with the Thumper
pillow while you read the latest issue of *Pulphouse*.

Want to mark off the date when your next issue will arrive?
Get the *Pulphouse* calendar featuring some of our favorite
Pulphouse cartoons!

Find all this and so much more at the *Pulphouse Fiction
Magazine* online store at:

http://pulphousemagazine.com

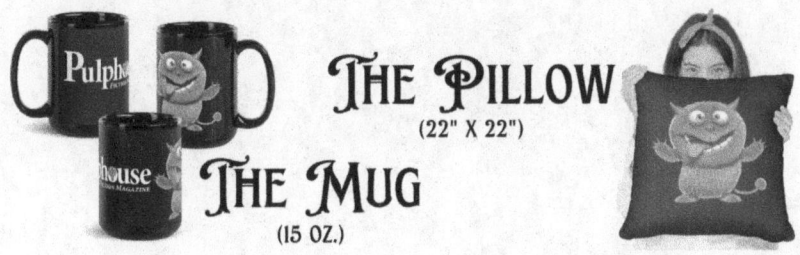

And say hi to Thumper while you're there.

THE HEART HAS REASONS

O'NEIL DE NOUX

I want Pulphouse Fiction Magazine *to cover many genres every issue. And that includes detective fiction. O'Neil De Noux is one of the best working short story writers of detective fiction in the business.*

His awards include The United Kingtom Short Story Prize, the Shamus Award for (for best private eye fiction), the Deringer Award (for excellence in mystery short fiction), and Police Book of the Year. Two of his stories have appeared in the prestigious Best American Mystery Stories annual anthology.

And O'Neil knows New Orleans because he was a homicide detective there. You can't go wrong finding and reading any of his novels or stories. And I feel very lucky to have someone of his skill at detective fiction.

THE HEART HAS REASONS

O'NEIL DE NOUX

For two days she came and sat under the WPA shelter in Cabrini Playground with her baby, sometimes rocking the infant, sometimes walking between the oaks and magnolias, back and forth. Sometimes she would sing. She came around nine a.m. and around lunchtime she'd reach into the paper bag she'd brought and nibble on a sandwich. After, she would cover her shoulder with a small pink blanket and nurse her baby beneath the blanket. Around five p.m., she would walk away, up Dauphine Street.

On the third morning the rain swept in, one of those all-day New Orleans rainstorms that started suddenly then built into monsoon proportions. The newspaper said to expect showers brought in by an atypical autumn cool front from Canada, which would finally break the heat wave that has lingered through the sizzling summer of 1948. I grabbed two umbrellas and found her huddled under the shelter.

"Come on," I told her, "come get out of the rain." I held out an umbrella. When she didn't take it immediately, I stood it against the wall and stepped away to give her some room. She looked younger up close, nineteen, maybe eighteen and stood about five-two, a thin girl with short, dark brown hair and darker brown eyes, all saucer-wide and blinking at me with genuine fear.

I took another step away from her, not wanting to tower over her with my six foot frame, and smiled as warmly as I could. "Please. Come take your baby out of the rain." I opened the second umbrella and handed it to her.

Slowly, a shaky white hand extended for the umbrella, those big eyes still staring at me. I took a step toward the edge of the shelter. A loud thunderclap caused us both to jump and the baby started crying.

I led the way back across the small playground, the umbrellas pretty useless in the deluge, and hurried through the brick and wrought iron fence to narrow Barracks Street, having to pause a moment to let a yellow cab pass. She moved carefully behind me and I held the door to my building open for her. I closed the umbrellas and started up the stairs for my apartment. "I'll bring towels down," I called back to her, then took the stairs two at a time.

Moving quickly, I grabbed two large towels from my bathroom, lighting the gas heater while I was in there and pulled the big terry-cloth robe I never wore from the closet, draping it over the bathroom door before leaving my apartment door open on the way out. She stood next to the smoky glass door of my office, rocking her baby, who had stopped crying. She still gave me that frightened look when I came down and extended the towels to her.

"Top of the stairs, take a left. My apartment door's open." I reached into my suit coat pocket and pulled out a business

4

card. "That's my office behind you. The number's on the card. Go upstairs. The heaters on in the bathroom and take your time. Lock yourself in. Call me if you need anything."

I shoved the towels at her and she took them with her free hand. I pressed the business card between her fingers as she moved away from my office door. She took a hesitant step for the stairs, stopped and watched me with hooded eyes now.

Stepping to my office door, I told her, "I'm Lucien Caye," and nodded at my name stenciled on the smoky glass door. "I'm a detective."

Her lower lip quivered, so I tried my warmest smile again. "Go on upstairs. You'll be safe up there. Lock yourself in."

The baby began to whine. She took in a deep breath and backed toward the bottom step. Glancing up the stairs, she said, "First door on the left?"

"It's open," I said as I stepped into my office. "I'll start up some eggs and bacon. I have a stove in here." I left the door open and returned to the row of windows along Barracks Street where I'd been watching her. A louder thunder clap shook the old building before two flashes of lightning danced over the rooftops of the French Quarter. The street was a mini-canal already, the storm washing the dust from my old gray, pre-war 1940 DeSoto coach parked against the curb.

"Bacon and eggs," I said aloud and turned back to the small kitchen area at the rear of my office. I had six eggs left in the small refrigerator, a half-slab of bacon and milk for the coffee. I sniffed the milk and it smelled OK.

I called my apartment before going up. She answered after the sixth ring with a hesitant, "Yes?"

"It's Lucien. Downstairs. I'm bringing up some bacon, eggs and coffee, OK?"

I heard her breathing.

"I'm the guy who got you outta the rain. Remember? Dark hair. Six feet tall. I brought an umbrella."

"The door's not locked," she said.

"OK. I'll be right up." When she didn't hang up immediately, I told her, "You can hang up now."

"All right." She did and I brought a heaping plate of breakfast and a mug of café-au-lait. I'd left my coat downstairs, along with my .38 revolver. Didn't want to spook her any more than she was already spooked.

She was sitting on the sofa, her baby sleeping next to her. In the terry-cloth robe, a towel wrapped around her wet hair like a swami, she looked like a kid, not a mother. The baby lay on its belly, wrapped in a towel. I went to my Formica kitchen table and put the food down, flipping on the light and telling her I'd be downstairs if she needed anything else.

"Is that a holster?" she asked, staring at my right hip.

"I told you I'm a detective." I kept moving toward the door, giving her a wide berth, hoping the fear in her eyes would subside.

"Thank you," she said, standing up, arms folded across her chest now.

I pointed down the hall beyond my bathroom. "There's a washer back there for your clothes and a clothesline out back, if it ever stops raining."

She nodded and said, "I'm Kaye Bishop." She looked down at her baby. "This is Donna."

I stopped just inside the door. "Nice to meet you Kaye. If you need to call anyone, you know where the phone is."

I hesitated in case she wanted to keep talking and she

surprised me with, "You're not how I would picture a detective."

"How's that?"

Her eyes, like chocolate agates, stared back at me. "You seem polite. Maybe too polite."

"You've been out there for three days. You all right?"

"We'll be fine when Charley comes for us."

"Charley?"

"Charley Rudabaugh. Donna's father. We're not married, yet. That's why I'm staying with the Ursulines."

Nuns. The Ursuline convent on Chartres Street. Oldest building in the Quarter. Only building which didn't burn in the two fires that engulfed the city in the Eighteenth Century, or so the story goes. For an instant I saw Kaye Bishop in a colonial costume, as a casket girl, labeled because they'd arrived in New Orleans with all their belongings in a single case that looked like a casket. Imported wives from France, daughters of impoverished families sent to the new world to marry the French settlers. The Ursulines took them under wing to make sure they were properly married before taken off by the early, rough settlers. Looks like they're still taking care of young girls.

"The church took us in." Her eyes were wet now. "We're waiting until Charley can get us a place."

Donna let out a little cry and Kaye scooped up her baby and moved to my mother's old rocking chair next to the French doors that opened to the wrought iron balcony wrapping around my building, along the second floor. As she rocked her baby, she reached up and unwrapped the towel on her head, shook out her hair and rubbed the towel through her hair.

The baby giggled and she giggled back. "You like that?" She shook her hair out again and the baby laughed. Turning to me, she said, "Can you get my purse? It's in the bathroom."

I brought it to her and she took out a brush and brushed out her short brown hair. Donna peeked up at me, hands swinging in small circles, legs kicking.

"She's a beautiful baby," I said backing away, not wanting to crowd them.

Kaye smiled at her daughter as she brushed her hair, the rocker moving now. I was about to ask if the eggs and bacon were OK when she started humming, then singing in a low voice, a song in French, a song that sat me down on my sofa.

My mother sang that song to me. I recognized the refrain... *"le coeur a ses raisons que la raison ne connait point."* Still don't know what it means. I wanted to ask Kaye but didn't want to interrupt her as she hummed part of the song and sang part.

I closed my eyes and listened. It was hard because I could hear my heart beating in my ears. When the singing stopped and I opened my eyes, Kaye was staring at me and I could see she wasn't afraid of me anymore.

———

Two hours later, I was about to call upstairs to suggest I go over and pick up Charley, bring him here when she called and said, "Could you get a message to Charley for me?"

"Sure."

"He's working at the Gulf station, Canal and Claiborne. He's a mechanic," she said with pride.

Slipping my blue suit coat back on, I looked out at the rain still falling on my DeSoto. It wasn't coming down as hard now but I took the umbrella anyway after I went back and slid my .38 back into its holster. I started to grab my tan fedora but left it on the coat rack. Hats just mess up my hair.

It took a good half hour to reach the station on a drive that normally took fifteen minutes. Every car in front of me drove so slowly, it was as if these people had never seen rain before in one of the wettest cities in the country. I resisted leaning on my horn for an old man wearing a hat two sizes too large for his pin head, wondering why he couldn't get his Cadillac out of first gear.

Forked lightning danced in the sky, right over the tan bricks of Charity Hospital towering a few blocks behind the Gulf station as I pulled in. The station stood out bright-white in the rain, illuminated by its lights normally on only at night. I parked outside the middle bay with the word "tires" above the doorway. The other bays, marked "lubrication" and "batteries" were filled with jacked-up vehicles.

Leaving the umbrella in my DeSoto, I jogged into the open bay and came face up with a hulking man holding a tire iron.

"Hi, I'm looking for Charley Rudabaugh."

He lifted the tire iron and took a menacing step toward me. I stumbled back, turning to my right as I reached under my coat for my revolver.

"Sam!" a voice boomed behind the man and he stopped but kept leering at me with angry eyes.

I kept the .38 against my leg as I took another step back to the edge of the open bay doors so he'd have to take two steps to get to me. I'd have to run or shoot him. Neither choice was a good one. A second hulking man, even bigger, came around the man with the tire iron. Both wore dark green coveralls with the orange Gulf Oil logos over their hearts.

The bigger man growled, "Who the hell are you?"

"Kaye Bishop sent me with a message for Charley."

"Kaye? Where is she?" He took a step toward me and I showed him my Smith and Wesson, but didn't point it at him.

"I'm a private detective. You wanna tell me what's goin' on?"

"You got an ID?"

Don't remember ever seeing Bogart, as Sam Spade or Philip Marlowe, showing his ID to anyone, but I had to do it— a lot. I reached into my coat pocket with my left hand and opened my credentials pouch for him and asked, "Where's Charley?"

The bigger man looked hard at my ID. "I'm Malone," he said. "Charley works for me. Where's Kaye?"

"At my office." I slipped my creds back into my coat pocket.

Malone turned his face to the side and spoke to his buddy with the tire iron. "He's too skinny to work for Joe. And his nose ain't been broke. Yet."

The man with the tire iron backed away, leaning against the fender of a Ford with its rear jacked up.

"I told you where Kaye is. Where's Charley?" I re-holstered my revolver but kept my distance.

"Don't trust the bastard," said the man with the tire iron.

I could see, in both sets of eyes, there was no way they were telling me anything. Maybe they'd tell Kaye. I suggested we get her on the phone. I stayed in the garage as Malone called my apartment from the office area. When he signaled for me to come in and get the phone, the first hulk finally put the tire iron down.

"Kaye?"

"Charley's in the hospital," she said excitedly. "Can you bring me to him?"

"I'll be right there." I hung up and looked at Malone. "You wanna tell me what happened now?"

Charley Rudabaugh was a good kid, a hard worker, but he borrowed money from the wrong man. Malone learned that tidbit that very morning when a goon came by with a sawed-off baseball bat and broke Charley's right arm.

"I was under a Buick and couldn't get out before the goon got away."

"The 'Joe' you thought I was working for?"

"No. A goon works for Joe Grosetto."

Malone explained Grosetto was a local loan shark. I asked where I could locate this shark but neither knew for sure. Charley would.

————

Kaye and Donna were waiting for me in the foyer of my building. I brought them out to the DeSoto under the umbrella and drove straight to Charity Hospital, parking at an empty meter outside the emergency room.

Charley Rudabaugh was about five-ten, thin build with curly light brown hair and green eyes. He smiled at Kaye and kissed Donna and finally noticed me standing behind them. His right arm in a fresh cast, Charley blinked and said, "Who are you?"

I let Kaye explain as she held his left hand, bouncing a gurgling Donna cradled in her free arm. He looked at me suspiciously, sizing me up, giving me that look a male gives another when he just showed up with his woman. When Kaye

11

finished, more nervous now, she asked Charley what happened to him.

He turned to her and his eyes softened. He took in a deep breath and said, "Haney." She became pale and I pulled a chair over for her to sit, then went back to the doorway.

"He didn't ask where I was?" asked Kaye.

Charley shook his head. "He just wanted the money."

Kaye's eyes teared up and she pressed her face against his left arm and cried. Charley's eyes filled too and he closed them but the tears leaked out, down his lean face. Donna's arms swung around in circles as she lay cradled and I waited until one of the adults looked at me.

It was Charley and I asked, "How much money are we talking about?"

"This doesn't concern you."

Kaye stopped crying now and wiped her face on the sheet before sitting up.

I tried a different tack. "What school didya' go to?" The old New Orleans handshake. This was no public school kid. He told me he went to Jesuit. I told him I went to Holy Cross. Two Catholic school boys who'd gone to rival schools.

"Your parents can't help?" Jesuit was expensive.

"They don't live here anymore. And don't even ask about Kaye's parents. This is our problem."

"Everyone needs help, sometimes."

"That's what you do? Some kinda guardian angel?"

I shook my head, thought about it a second and said, "Actually, it's what I do most of the time. Help people figure things out."

"We can't afford a private-eye."

I tried still another tack. "How do I find this Grosetto? This Haney?"

Charley shook his head. Kaye wouldn't meet my eyes so I left them alone, went out in to the waiting area. Ten minutes later a blond-headed doctor went in, then a nurse. I caught the doctor on the way out. It was a simple fracture of both bones, the radius and ulna between wrist and elbow.

"It was a blunt instrument, officer," the doctor said. "Says he fell but something struck that arm."

I thanked the doc without correcting him that I wasn't a cop. The nurse was obviously finishing up, telling them how Charley had to move on soon as the cast was hard. Kaye turned her red eyes to me and I took in a deep breath. "I'll take you to the Ursulines, OK?"

Her shoulders sank. I turned to Charley. "So where have you been staying?"

"He's been sleeping at the Gulf station," Kaye said.

He shot her a worried look.

"They don't know," Kaye added. "He stays late to lock up and sleeps inside, opens in the morning."

I put my proposition to them to use my apartment and stepped out for them to discuss it, gave them another ten minutes before walking back in. Kaye shot me a nervous smile, holding Donna up now, the baby smiling too as her mother jiggled her.

I looked at Charley who asked, "I just wanna know why you're doing this."

"How old are you, Charley?"

"Twenty. And Kaye's eighteen. We're both adults now."

I nodded slowly and said, "I watched a young mother and her baby spend three days in that playground, avoiding the kids when they came, keeping to themselves until the rain blew in. I've got two apartments, one converted into an office downstairs with a sofa bed, kitchen and bath. I've slept down there before. You got a better offer?"

———

Charley and Kaye wouldn't volunteer any information about Grosetto and Haney and there was no way Malone and his tire-iron friend were going to be much help. But I knew who would. He was in too, sitting behind his worn government-issue gray metal desk, in a government-issue gray desk chair in a small office with gray walls lined with mug shots, wanted posters and an electric clock that surprisingly had the correct time.

Detective Eddie Sullivan had lost more of his red hair, making up for it with an old-fashioned handle-bar moustache. Grinning at me as I stepped up to his desk, he said, "I was about to get a bite."

"Me too."

So I bought him lunch around the corner from the First Precinct house on South Saratoga Street at Jilly's Grill. Hamburgers, French fries, coffee and a wedge of apple pie for my large friend. Sullivan was my height exactly but out-weighed me by a hundred pounds, mostly flab.

Eddie Sullivan was the Bunco Squad for the First Precinct, since his partner retired, without a replacement in sight. He handled con artists, forgers, loan sharks and the pawn shop detail, checking lists of pawned items against the master list of stolen articles reported to police. I waited until he'd wolfed down his burger and fries and was starting in on his slab of pie before bringing up Grosetto and Haney. He nodded and told me he knew both.

"Grosetto's a typical Guinea, short, olive-skinned, pencil thin moustache, weighs about a hundred pounds soaking wet. Haney is black Irish, big, goofy-looking. Typical bully." He stuffed another chunk of pie into his mouth.

"Grosetto? He mobbed up?"

Sullivan shook his head. "He wishes but he ain't Sicilian. I think he's Napolitano or just some ordinary Wop. You got someone willin' to file charges against these bums?

"Maybe. I need to know where they hang out."

"Easy. Rooms above the Blue Gym. Canal and Galvez."

I knew the place and hurried to finish my meal as Sullivan ordered a second wedge of pie. He managed to say, between mouthfuls, "I'd go with you but I gotta be in court at one o'clock. Drop me by the court house?"

As he climbed out of my DeSoto in front of the hulking, gray Criminal Courts Building, Tulane and Broad Avenues, he thanked me for lunch, adding, "See if you can talk your friend into pressing charges. I could use a good collar."

"I'll try."

The Blue Gym was hard to miss, sitting on the downtown side of Canal and Galvez Streets. Painted bright blue, it stood three stories high, the bottom two stories an open gym with six boxing rings inside, smelling of sweat, blood and cigar smoke. I weaved my way through a haze of smoke to a back stairs and went up to a narrow hall that

15

smelled like cooked fish. A thin man in boxing shorts came rushing out of a door and almost bumped into me.

"Oh, 'scuse me," he said.

"I'm looking for Grosetto."

He pointed to the door he'd just exited and rushed off. I reached back and unsnapped the trigger guard on the holster of my Smith and Wesson before stepping through the open door to spot a smallish man behind a beat-up wooden desk. The man glared at me with hard brown eyes, trying to look tough, hard to do when he stood up and topped off at maybe five-three and skinny as a stickman. He wore a sharkskin lime green suit.

"Who the hell are you?" he snarled from the right side of his tiny mouth.

I stepped up, keeping an eye on his hands in case he tried something stupid and said, "How much does Charley Rudabaugh owe you?"

"Huh?"

"How much?" I kept my voice even, without a hint of emotion.

The beady eyes examined me, up and down, then he sat and said, "You ain't Italian. What are you? Some kinda Mexican?"

I wasn't about to tell this jerk I'm half French, half Spanish, so I told him, "I'm the man with the money. You want your money, tell me how much Charley owes you."

"Three hundred and fifty. Tomorrow it's gonna be four hundred."

"I'll be right back." And I didn't look back as I strolled out, making it to the nearest branch of the Whitney Bank before it closed. My bank accounts, I have a saving account now, were both in good shape after the Duponceau Case. As I stood in the teller line, I remembered the salient facts that brought such money into my possession—

It was a probate matter. When it got slow, I'd go over to civil court, pick up an inheritance case. This one was a search for any descendants of a recently deceased uptown matron. Flat fee for my work. If I found someone, they got the inheritance, if not, the state got it. I'd worked a dozen before and never found anyone until I found Peter Duponceau, a fellow WWII vet, in a VA Hospital in Providence, Rhode Island.

Not long after I caught a bullet from a Nazi sniper at Monte Cassino, he collected a chest full of shrapnel from a Japanese bombardment on a small island called Saipan. Peter was the grandson of the recently deceased uptown matron. His mother was also deceased. When I met him to confirm his inheritance, he was back in the hospital for yet another operation. At least the last months of his life were lived in luxury in a mansion overlooking Audubon Park. He left most of his estate to several local VFW chapters and ten percent to Lucien Caye, Esquire. When the certified check arrived, I contemplated getting an armored car to drive me to the bank. I couldn't make that much money in five years, unless I robbed a bank or two.

———

G rosetto was back behind his desk but there was an addition to the room, a hulking man standing six-four, outweighing me by a good hundred pounds of what looked like grizzle, with a thick mane of unruly black hair and a ruddy complexion. He wore a rumpled brown suit as he stared at me with dull, brown eyes, Mississippi River water brown. My Irish friend Sullivan described Haney as black Irish, probably descended from the Spanish of the Great Armada, the ones who weren't drowned by the English. The ones who took the prevailing winds, beaching their ships along the Irish coast to be taken in by fellow Catholics to later breed with the locals. I would have given Haney only a cursory look, except I didn't expect he'd be so young, early twenties maybe.

Stepping up to the desk, I dropped the bank envelope in front of Grosetto. "Rudabaugh sign anything? Promissory note? IOU?" I knew better but asked anyway.

Grosetto picked up the envelope and counted the money, nodding when he was finished. I turned to Haney. "You still have that baseball bat?"

He looked at Grosetto for an answer and then looked back and I could see he wasn't all there.

"Try that stunt again and I'll put two in your head. And I'll get away with it."

"Alls I want is the girl," Haney said.

"What?"

He looked down at his feet, all shy-like and said, "I seen her," looking up now with those dull eyes, "*Real* pretty." He followed with a childlike chuckle.

I turned back to Grosetto, "Better let him in on the real world."

Grosetto was smiling now, or trying to with that crooked mouth. "He usually gets what he wants."

"Not this time," I said.

No use arguing with idiots. When I got back to my office, I located my blackjack, a chunk of lead attached to a thick spring, covered with black leather, brand named the Bighorn because it allegedly could cold-cock a charging bighorn ram. I only used it twice back when I was a patrolman and it worked well enough to incapacitate bigger, combative men. Then I put away my .38 and brought out my army issue Colt .45 caliber automatic and loaded it, switching holsters now. I needed something with stopping power.

I called upstairs and Kaye answered, telling me the baby and Charley were asleep.

"I need to get a couple things, OK?"

She let me in and I quickly packed a suitcase with essentials, grabbed a couple suits and fresh shirts. Before stepping out, I waved her over and we whispered in the hall. I told her they owed Grosetto nothing. How? I told her someone had given me a lot of money and now I was giving them some.

"Charley won't stand for it. We'll pay you back."

I shrugged, then watched her eyes as I told her I'd met Haney. She blanched, so I followed it with, "Back at Charity, why did you ask Charley if Haney asked where you were?"

She took a step back, crossed her arms and said, "Haney's my half-brother."

———

Sitting at my desk in my dark office, I watched the rain finally taper off.

"What about your parents?" I'd asked Kaye up in the hall. She told me her father was dead and her mother had abandoned her when she was five and wouldn't say anything else about the matter, not even who'd raised her.

I was thinking—at least they were safe for now—just as I

spotted Haney standing next to the playground fence across the street. Didn't take him long to find us. He stood there for a good ten minutes before coming across the street. I expected the baseball bat, not the revolver stuck in the waistband of his suit pants as he stepped in the foyer of my building. I'd moved into the shadows next to the stairs, blackjack in my left hand. Slowly, I eased my right hand back to my .45 as he saw me and said softly, "Where is she?"

The sound of squealing tires behind him made him look over his shoulder. When he looked back I had my .45 pointed at his face and said, "That'll be the cavalry."

Two uniforms alighted from the black prowl car and came into the building with their guns out. It was Williams and Jeanfreau, both rookies when I was at the Third Precinct. I lowered my weapon. "He's got a gun in his waistband."

Williams snatched Haney's revolver and Jeanfreau cuffed him and dragged him out.

"Aggravated Assault, right?" Williams checked with me for the charge.

"Yeah. Hopefully he's a convicted felon." A felon with a firearm would hold Haney for quite a while.

"Thanks," I called out to my old compadres. Williams called back, "Your call broke up the sergeant's poker game. But only for a while."

———

Charley sat shirtless at my kitchen table holding Donna with his good arm, Kaye in my terry cloth robe again, getting us coffee, them looking like a family now and I had to tell them about Haney. Kaye blanched at the news; Charley just nodded while Donna gurgled.

"How close are you?" I asked.

"I'm not even sure he's my half-brother," Kaye answered. "He claims to be. Claims my dad was his father. I never met him until he showed up at the hospital when Donna was born." She didn't volunteer anymore and I didn't want to cross-examine her, sitting at my table, all three adults sipping coffee which wasn't bad and I'm picky about my coffee.

I turned to Charley and said, "We need to press charges against Grosetto. I'll back you and we'll put the slime-ball away. My buddy Detective Sullivan is chomping at the bit to nail him."

Charley shook his head and told me, in careful, low tones how he wanted Grosetto and Haney and all of it behind him, how he was going to pay me back whatever it cost me. I tried for the next half hour, but there was no changing his mind. He said he didn't want to be looking over his shoulder for the rest of his life. God, he was so young.

The coffee kept me up a little while, but the rain came back that night, slapping against my office windows as I lay on my sofa-bed. Why was I lying there? Why wasn't I out on the town, dancing with a long tall blonde in a slinky dress? Maybe bringing her here or going to her place and helping her slip into something more comfortable, like my arms.

I knew the answer. It was upstairs with those kids, so I lay waiting for trouble to return, knowing it would.

Arriving at the Criminal Courts Building early, I searched the docket for Haney's name, wanting to get a word in with the judge before his arraignment. When I couldn't find his name, the acid in my stomach churned. I snatched up a pay phone in the lobby and called parish prison, speaking to the shift lieutenant who took his time, but looked up the name for me.

"Haney. Yeah. Bonded out four-thirty a.m."

I asked more questions and got the obvious answers, a friendly judge and a friendlier bail bondsman had Haney out before sunrise. The only surprise was that Haney had only two previous arrests, both misdemeanors, no convictions.

I should have gotten a speeding ticket on the way home, but no one was paying attention. Catching my breath when I reached the top of the stairs, I tapped lightly on the door. Even a bachelor knows better than to ring a doorbell with a baby inside. Kaye answered and I let out a relieved sigh, which disappeared immediately when she told me Charley wasn't there.

"Where'd he go?"

"To work. Malone picked him up." Her eyebrows furrowed when she saw the worried look in my eyes. I pointed to the phone and she opened the door wider, telling me, "Malone said a one-armed Charley was better than any of his other mechanics."

She knew the number by heart and I dialed. Malone answered after the fifth ring and I warned him about Haney being out of jail.

"Didn't know he was in jail."

"Well, he had a gun last night, so be on the lookout."

Then I called Sullivan to make sure the patrol boys did a drive-by at the Gulf Station before I went to see Grosetto.

————

He was behind the desk wearing the same lime green suit, sporting that same crooked slimy grin when I walked in on him, the place reeking of fish again.

"Where's Haney?"

Grosetto tried growling, which only made him look like a randy terrier, instead of a gangster. His hands dropped below the desk top and I turned my left shoulder to him, pulling out my .45, letting him get a look at it.

"Put your hands back on your desk and they better be empty."

"Who da' heller you comin' in here, tellin' me what to do?"

"Where's Haney?"

He tried smiling but it looked more like a grimace. "I'm glad you come by. You needa tell Charley he owes another fifty. I, how you put it, miscalculated the amount." This time it was a smile, sickly, showing off yellowed-teeth.

I shot his telephone, watched it bounce high, slam against the back wall, the loud report of my .45 echoing in my ears. Pointing it at his face now, I said. "Put your hands back on your desk."

He did, his eyes bulging now. I backed up and locked the door behind me and came back to the desk as I holstered my weapon, slammed both hands against the desk, shoving it across the linoleum floor with him and his chair behind, pinning him against the wall.

"Tell Haney I'm looking for him."

Three boxers and two trainers were in the narrow hall. I opened my coat and showed them the .45 and they backed away cautiously, none of them saying anything until I started through the gym. A couple brave ones cursed me behind my back, but kept their distance.

———

I figured Haney was loony enough to come by but it was Grosetto, just before midnight. He wore a gray dress shirt and black pants, hands high as he stepped into my building's foyer. I was sitting in darkness, half-way up the stairs, sitting in my shirt and pants with my .45 in my right hand.

"That you?" he called out when I told him to freeze. I'd unscrewed the hall light.

"What do you want?"

"I come to tell you somethin'."

I went and patted him down, closed and locked the building door then shoved him into my office, leaving the door open. He smelled like cigarette smoke and stale beer. I made him stand still as I moved to my desk and leaned against it.

"All right, what is it?"

"I made a mistake. Charley don't owe me nothin'."

"Good."

He tried smiling again, but it still didn't work. "I checked on you. You got some rep. You know. War hero. Ex-cop. Bad when you gotta be bad." He looked around my office for a second. "You check up on me?"

"In the dictionary. Under scum bag."

"You funny. You owe me a phone, you know."

Maybe it was the twitch in his eye or the way he sucked in a breath when I heard it, a thump upstairs. Grosetto should never play poker. It was in his eyes and I was on him in three long strides, slamming the .45 against his pointed head, tumbling him out of my way.

I took the stairs three at a time, reaching the top of the stairs as a gunshot rang out. My apartment door was open and a woman's screaming voice echoed as I ran in, scene registering as I swung my .45 toward the figure standing with a gun in hand. The gun turned toward me and I fired twice, Haney bouncing on his toes as the rounds punched his chest. The gun dropped and he fell straight back, head ricocheting off an end table.

Kaye, with Donna in her arms, moved for Charley as he lay on the kitchen floor, a circle of bright red blood under him. Holstering my weapon, I leaped toward them as Kaye cradled his head in her arms. He was conscious, a neat hole in his lower abdomen, blood oozing through his white undershirt. I jumped back to the phone and called for an ambulance. When I turned back, Charley was trying to sit up.

"Don't!" I jumped into the kitchen, snatched an ice tray from the freezer, broke up the ice, wrapped it in a dishcloth and got Kaye out of the way with Donna screeching now. I pressed the ice against the wound and told Charley to keep calm, the ambulance would be right there. Then I remembered I'd locked the foyer door and had to go down for it.

Charley was still conscious when they rolled him out with Kaye and Donna in tow. Williams and Jeanfreau had accompanied the ambulance and used my phone to call the detectives.

"What'd you shoot him with?" Williams asked, pointing to

the two large holes around Haney's heart. I pointed to my .45 which I'd put on the kitchen counter before they came in.

It was then I remembered Grosetto and brought Williams down to my office. The little greaseball was just coming around and Williams slapped his cuffs on him and brought him up to have a look at Haney. The dead man looked younger in death in a yellow shirt and dungarees, his eyes even duller now, his face flaccid. To me he looked like an eighth-grader trying to pass himself off at a high school. His shoes were tied in double knots as if his mom had made sure they wouldn't come undone.

It took the detectives forty minutes to get there. I made coffee for all and was on my second cup when Lt. Frenchy Capdeville strolled in, trailing cigarette smoke, a rookie dick at his heels. Frenchy needed a haircut badly, his black hair in loose curls over the collar of his brown suit.

His rookie partner had tried a pencil-thin moustache, like Frenchy's, but his was lopsided. "Joe Sparks," Frenchy introduced him to me. Sparks, also in a brown suit, was sharp enough to keep quiet and let Frenchy run the show, which he did, quickly and efficiently.

After the coroner's men took Haney away, they took me and Grosetto to the Detective Bureau, Frenchy calling in Eddie Sullivan. While they booked Grosetto, I gave a formal statement about the first man I'd shot since the war. Self-defense, defined in Louisiana's Napoleonic Code Law was—justifiable homicide.

———

I t didn't take a detective to discover how Haney had come in the back way, through the broken fence of the building next door, across the back courtyard and up the rear fire escape to break the hallway window.

"How'd he get in the apartment?" I asked Kaye as we sat in the hall at Charity Hospital the following morning, while Charley slept in the recovery ward. Dark circles around her eyes, she looked pale as she rocked Donna slowly. Thankfully the baby was asleep.

"I heard scratching against the door and thought it was the cat, the black one that's always around."

"Did he say anything?"

"No. He just shoved past me and shot Charley. Then he stood there looking at me."

A nurse came out of Charley's room and said, "He's awake now."

I didn't go in. I went back home to look up my landlord.

———

C harley Rudabaugh spent six days in the hospital. When I brought him home and walked him past my apartment door to the rear apartment, he balked until Kaye opened the door and smiled at him.

"What's going on?"

Kaye pulled him in and I stood in the doorway, amazed at what she'd done with the place in a few days. It came furnished but she'd brightened it up, replaced the dark curtains with yellow ones, the place looking spotless. Donna, lying on her back in a playpen in the center of the living room was trying to play with a rubber duck, slapping at it and gurgling.

It took Charley a good minute to take in the scene as Kaye eased up and hugged him.

"Here's the deal," I told them over coffee at their kitchen table. "The landlord gave us a break on the place. I'm fronting y'all the money. You don't have to pay me back, but if you insist, you can, but get on your feet first." I'd just put any money they gave me in a bank account for Donna's education.

Then I explained about how it really wasn't my money. It had been a gift and I was sharing it. "Everyone needs help sometimes. And you two have had a bad time recently."

I could see Charley was still confused, but not Kaye, beaming at him, paying little if any attention to me. I thanked her for the coffee and stood up to leave. Charley's eyes narrowed as he asked, "I understand what you say, but it's just hard to figure you ain't got some kinda motive. Everybody does."

I started for the door, turned and said, "Sometimes things are exactly as they appear to be."

Kaye moved to her daughter and began humming that same song, repeating the line in French again, *"le coeur a..."*

"What is that?" I had to ask.

"It's the reason you're doing all this." She smiled at me, looking like a school kid in her white shirt and jeans. "An old French saying that goes, 'The heart has reasons of which reason knows nothing'." She smiled down at her baby.

It wasn't until later, as I sat in my mother's rocker looking out the open French doors of my apartment, out at the dark roofs of the Quarter with the moon beaming overhead, that I heard my mother's voice back when she was young, a voice I haven't heard for so long, as she sang, *"le coeur a..."*

Then it hit me.

The heart has reasons of which reason knows nothing. Kaye hadn't meant just me. It cut both ways. She'd also meant Haney and I felt the hair on the back of my neck standing up.

WITH LOVE IN THEIR HEARTS

ROBERT JESCHONEK

Robert Jeschonek continues his streak of being in every issue of Pulphouse Fiction Magazine.

The moment I started reading this story, I knew I was in for a very twisted journey with lots of meaning and emotion. I was not wrong.

Robert's stories have appeared in dozens of magazines and he has published dozens of novels as well. He has even worked for DC Comics and early in his career sold me a couple stories when I was editing for Star Trek at Pocket Books. He seems to be able to do it all. And to see all the amazing projects he has done, check out his website at https://www.robertjeschonek.com/

WITH LOVE IN THEIR HEARTS

ROBERT JESCHONEK

"I love you!" Hissing the words through the blood in my mouth, I lunge at my opponent. And I *mean* those words with all my heart—I *have* to—even as I swipe my dagger across his chest.

As he dances back out of reach, a line of red opens up where I cut him. His dirty, bearded face clouds…then quickly clears. "I love you *more*!" He smiles as he leaps at me with both fists forward, aiming them like a battering ram at my face.

Beaming with all the affection I can muster, all the true sweet regard for my friendly fellow man, I spin around out of his way and tag him again with the dagger, plugging the blade deep in his left kidney.

Howling, he stumbles into the thick-trunked oak that was just at my back. He takes it headfirst and bounces off, weaving drunkenly in the mud.

"Friend warrior." This is how I finish him, all sweetness and light. Without the *slightest* shred of darkness in my heart.

"You are like unto the finest flower in the brightest sunbeam on the loveliest day in all the year." Darting to one side, I duck down and recover the sword I dropped earlier in this battle— dearest Eros. "God bless you for bringing such *joy* to my life."

With that, I swing the sword up, then down and through his neck with a perfect, practiced stroke.

So good am I at this that not a *trace* of hatred or savage satisfaction punctuates the moment when his head separates from his shoulders and plops into the muck.

Breathing hard, I scan my surroundings. I see the bodies of the three men I've killed, sprawled in various bloody contortions...and the body of Vicka, my partner on the road until now, whom they killed before I could kill them first.

That is what love can accomplish. Its power is arrayed around me for all to behold.

———

Moving swiftly lest another patrol comes my way too soon, I secure my beaten black body armor, then retrieve and put on my battered helmet with the old red-white-and-blue banner etched into the hard plastic. I retrieve my motorbike, too...but the front tire has been slashed, and it won't start. I guess I can't complain; it's over a century old, and I've gotten a lot of use out of it until now.

"Go with God, fair machine." I drop it in the muck, grab my dagger from the dead man's kidney, and set off at a brisk jog through the woods. The autumn sun is closing in on the horizon, and I need to make my destination by nightfall.

Everything is riding on the completion of my mission. All my people down in Burytown are counting on me to succeed.

Though it is hard to imagine I *can* succeed this time. The killing of men and women has always come easy to me. It is *that* very inclination that could make this new mission such a challenge.

Heart pounding, I run through the mud, brush, and leaves, ever up along the steep contour of the mountainside. This part of what was once known as the state of Pennsylvania is full of such mountains—the *Alleghenies*, as we call them yet today. They have been my home for all five and twenty years of my life, and navigating them is second nature to me.

Reading the wind and the angle of the sun, I know I'm not far from my goal. In spite of the best efforts of my attackers, I will reach my destination, though what happens after that, I cannot say.

Finally, I burst from the woods and find myself at the edge of the old road. I also find myself face to face with two men in camouflage body armor, wielding six-guns.

Slowly, I take off the helmet. "Greetings to you both."

"Hail and well met, good stranger!" The one doing the talking has the biggest, friendliest smile...and the steadiest grip on his revolver. "State your name and purpose, that we may love you all the better!"

Instinctively, I meet his gaze with the most genuine grin I can muster. "I am Sir Gardner Schell of Burytown," I tell them. "I have come to meet my bride."

———————

Expected as I am, the sentinels holster their guns and lead me through the barricades blocking the road. On the other side, my destination awaits—a place I've only visited a handful of times, though Burytown lies but seven miles to the west of it.

The building looks for all the world like an old ocean liner (the kind I've seen only in photos), complete with decks, portholes, and a pair of big smokestacks on the roof, angled toward the stern. It is as if, by some miracle, a seagoing vessel has been stranded in the heights of a mountain range, along the curve of a once-great highway that has seen better days.

GRAND VIEW SHIP HOTEL. That's the old name of it, painted in big black letters on the side of the ship facing the road. SEE 3 STATES AND 7 COUNTIES. That's painted on the prow. Armor plating has been added all around, but those words out of history remain.

The *real* name, the one it's known by now, is not painted anywhere. But ask anyone within fifty miles of here if they know of Kendall's Keep, and they will point you right to it. Everyone who uses this stretch of road—known in olden times as the Highway of Lincoln—must pay a toll to Kendall's men to pass this point.

"What took you so long?" Lord Rubicon Kendall strides out of the keep in a white sea captain's uniform, looking hale and hearty and overly friendly. A sword hangs at either hip, plus a long rifle at his back, and rightly so; his clan is at war. "You were expected *this morning,* good sir knight."

"If not for the *second* ambush, I most certainly would have been here sooner. And Vicka, my late retainer, as well." I point at the path that I traveled up the slope. "The *Loved Ones* grow ever bolder, my Lord."

Rubicon grins through his neatly trimmed ebony mustache and goatee. "It is a delight we have in common, yes? Your

people down in Burytown have been *especially* showered with
their affections, have they not?"

"Such a blessing." I say it stiffly, though I manage a smile.
The siege of Burytown is my whole reason for being here. An
alliance with Rubicon's clan would give us the punch we need
to break the siege and lay our friends the Loved Ones to rest
for good.

Though such an alliance does not come without a price.

"I am in your hands, my Lord." I bow my head and spread
my arms. "Assuming our pact yet stands."

"It does. My Lady Kendall, God rest her soul, had people
in Burytown. I am only too happy to offer you this chance."
He lays a hand on my shoulder. "*If* you are ready for the challenge, Sir Gardner."

"I would not be here if I were not."

"Well said." Rubicon nods sagely, peering into my eyes
with the focus of a hawk. "And would you accept the guidance of an advisor in this quest of yours? He was of much help
when *I* was in your shoes."

"Thank you, my Lord, but that won't be necessary."

Rubicon cocks his head to one side, looking amused. "May
he provide a *benediction*, at least?"

Before I can answer, an old man rises on the main deck on
the second level of the ship/keep and clears his throat. "Let us
pray," he calls down to us. Like Rubicon, he wears a uniform,
though the pieces don't go together well: white cap, black
jacket, red ascot, lemon trousers.

Confidentially, Rubicon leans over and whispers to me.
"Bon Cloister up there will perform the ceremony, you know.
If there *is* one."

"In the century since the Great Collapse," says Cloister,

"only *love* has sustained we few survivors. As this young knight stands on the precipice of the greatest struggle of all— holy wedlock—we pray that he may turn to *another* face of love and do what we all know he *must* do to succeed."

"Amen." Grinning, Rubicon smacks me on the back.

"Times a million," says Cloister as he digs out a pipe and lights it with a hellaciously long furnace match.

———

"**H**ere we are." Rubicon leads me past armed guards into the keep, then down a short hallway. "Have a seat in the Coral Room, Sir Gardner."

We enter a room with turquoise walls and red-rimmed portholes. A polished wooden bar occupies most of one side, with a black-cushioned elbow rest and pink-upholstered barstools with backs. Dusty glasses and bottles line shelves behind the bar, glinting in the last flickers of daylight slipping in from the windows in the dining room next door.

I sit on a long red bench against the opposite wall. A knight must *never* sit with his back to the door, as I have learned the hard way.

Just then, I hear footsteps—hard shoes descending a staircase.

"Here she comes." Rubicon smiles and bounces on the balls of his feet. "Good luck to you." He winks and whispers that last.

My heart beats fast as the footsteps approach down the hallway. I have fought a thousand battles, but this is new ground for me.

"Sir Gardner." Rubicon steps aside and gestures at the doorway. "I introduce my daughter, Listy Kendall."

I rise as she enters the room. Never in my life have I seen anyone so *beautiful*.

Listy curtsies. "Sir Gardner." She is in her early twenties, with all the firmness of youth in her pale, porcelain skin. Loose, dark curls frame an oval face with lively eyes, delicate nose, and full red lips. I can see from the fall of her long, creamy gown that her body is perfectly sculpted, bust and hips swelling pleasingly above and below a slender waist.

I manage a bow, but words fail me. Entranced, I can but stare as she watches and waits, smiling.

Rubicon raises an eyebrow and gestures at the bar. "Perhaps you might like a drink, Sir Gardner?"

His question barely registers. I am spellbound.

"My father has pledged my hand to you, good knight," says Listy. "It might do us well to converse upon this betrothal, don't you think?"

Her voice, as soft and flowing as the song of a meadowlark, freezes me further. I am drawn to her, mesmerized as I have never been before—yet locked down as if shackled and gagged. A man of action I have always been, but now I am turned to stone.

And none of it makes any sense to me.

"Ha. I wondered if this might happen." Rubicon walks over and squeezes my shoulder. "Perhaps some time with Bon Cloister might not be a bad idea *after* all, sir knight."

———

F resh air does me some good. As I stand at the railing of the keep's main deck and watch the sun set, my wits slowly return to me.

Without invitation, Bon Cloister shuffles over to stand beside me, lighting a fresh pipeful of tobacco. Up close, I see how withered he is, how ancient in his shabby hodge-podge uniform.

"What is the Story of Love, Sir Gardner?" He puffs twice on the pipe, then exhales sweet cherry-smelling smoke from his nose. "Tell me how love as we know it came to be."

Everyone knows this story, but I humor him. I'm embarrassed about what happened in the Coral Room and eager to make things right.

"One of the plagues of the Great Collapse in the Twenty-First Century was *The Commandment*," I tell him. "Scientists unleashed a contagion to rewrite human DNA and bring about peace on Earth."

"How so?"

"People became physically unable to harm others out of hatred or anger. This was in fulfillment of Jesus Christ's commandment to love thy neighbor as thyself."

"Indeed." Smoke from Cloister's pipe drifts out over the vast landscape sprawling beyond the mountain. The setting sun casts blazing light over the acres of trees in their red, gold, and orange autumn finery. "And how did that work out when the *other* plagues struck, and civilization *collapsed?*"

"It made it nearly impossible to fight for survival."

Cloister smiles. "And so we learned to fight—to *kill* if need be—the only way we *could*. With *love* in our hearts." He pulls the pipe from his mouth. "And we got very *good* at it, didn't we? The love-that-kills?"

I nod.

"*But!*" Cloister jabs the pipe stem at me. "What happens when we get so *good* at it, we forget what it's like to feel the *love-that-cher-ishes*? For some, especially the more...*accomplished* warriors, like yourself...this can sometimes lead to profound...*disharmonies.*"

"The love-that-cherishes?" I scowl.

"Caring for someone so much that we *don't* want to damage or murder them," says Cloister. "Feeling an attraction so *real* and *profound* that we want to join with the other person in a multitude of ways."

The song of the katydids buzzing in the trees makes more sense to me than what he's saying. "Is that even possible?" I ask.

Cloister narrows his eyes. "Do you *want* it to be?"

I think of my people in Burytown, who are depending on me. I think also of that beautiful girl in the Coral Room, and the way she seemed to glow when I gazed at her. "Yes." I whisper the word. "But how?"

"Righteous discipline." Cloister clenches his right hand. "And self-control. You must reach deep within yourself and change the love-that-kills to the love-that-cherishes...but *only* for this one person, your bride. For all others, especially those who threaten kith or kin..." He unclenches his hand and draws the edge of it across his throat like the blade of a knife.

Frustrated, I close my eyes and clench my teeth. I feel like going over the rail and running off into the night with Eros in hand, ready to love all comers. That, at least, would not be like the great unknown I now face.

"So many feelings…" I grip the rail hard. "What if I can't *master* them, Bon?"

"Then your bargain with Lord Kendall will never be consummated." Cloister puts the pipe back in his mouth and puffs on it. "For neither he nor Listy herself shall brook a union where there is no *true* affection."

"Damn." I toss my head as if I'm trying to wake myself from a terrible dream. "I don't even know where to start."

"There are some mental drills that might help." Cloister pats me on the back. "Perhaps we can get you ready for tomorrow morning."

"What's happening tomorrow morning?"

"Your first date," says Cloister. "Also, if all goes well, your marriage proposal."

———

I wake, as always, before dawn, springing to full alertness with all the force of old habits. Sleeping too soundly or late can get you killed in the field, after all.

I wash up in a basin of tepid water in my room, then dry and dress. Looking out the window, I see it's still dark outside…but won't be for long. I am early for this morning's meeting, which is just how I like to be.

In this, Listy Kendall and I have something in common. When I arrive on the main deck, she is waiting there already, setting up an easel and palette of paints by the light of an oil lamp.

"Good morning," she says, waving a brush in my direction. "I trust you slept well, Sir Gardner?"

My heart races, and words catch in my throat. She looks as

lovely as she did when we first met, in the Coral Room...and I feel just as frozen, just as shackled by conflicting emotions.

But then I run one of the exercises Cloister taught me, repeating these words in my head: *Kindness is not always hatred. Hatred is not always kindness.*

Something about that simple repetition weakens the bonds just enough for me to speak. "Yes, I did sleep well." It isn't much, but I consider it a victory.

"Glad to hear it." She strokes a rich red base on the canvas as the sky begins to brighten. "You don't mind if I paint, do you? It's going to be such a lovely autumn morning."

"Not at all." I can barely force out the words. The way her lacy white blouse clings to her breasts, and her black britches hug the curves of her hips and bottom, I have trouble focusing on the conversation at hand.

"So, Sir Gardner." Listy swirls in white with the red, stirring it into a deep pink color. "What hobbies do *you* have?"

C-Love, not K-Love. That's another exercise Cloister taught me. *C-Love, not K-Love,* as in *the love-that-cherishes,* not *the love-that-kills.* "Well..." I fight for focus. "I sharpen my *blades* in my spare time. And train younger knights in battlefield techniques."

"Sounds more like *work* to me." Listy tips her head and gives me a funny look out of the corner of her eye. "Do you ever court *maidens,* I wonder?"

I feel myself blush. *C-Love, not K-Love. C-Love, not K-Love.* "I, uh...no, I..." In spite of the mantra, my brain locks up, and my voice trails off.

"Oh, look." Listy pauses in dabbing at the canvas and gazes out at the scenery, mouth open in wonder. "Come here, Sir Gardner."

I step up beside her, following her gaze with my own. The sky, by now, is fairly bright, so the vast gulf below is awash in predawn light—but it appears not at all as it did the evening before. Everywhere I look, instead of swaths of colorful trees and distant green fields, I see an expanse of mist blanketing everything.

"I love when it's like this." Her voice is low and soft. "My grandfather used to say it was like an ocean of cloud out there. He half-expected to see a dolphin jump out of it, he said." She bumps my arm with her elbow. "Not that he was *biased*, living in a ship on the mountain and all."

"Three states, seven counties." Lost in the view, I get my voice back. "It's as if they've disappeared."

"They're still out there. They always are." Her elbow nudges my arm again. "You just can't *see* them."

Staring into that milky abyss, I let my imagination run away with me—something I rarely do. "It's more like Heaven than an ocean," I say, though I've only ever seen photos of oceans or paintings of Heaven.

When a bird pops out of the mist nearby, it startles me back to reality. I become fully aware of Listy's body next to mine, her elbow against my arm...and that triggers the kind of reaction I had before.

Even as it happens, I hate myself for it. Burytown is in dire need; am I so *damaged* that I can't at least *bluff* my way through the one chance I have to *save* it?

Yes, apparently.

Stumbling back from the railing, I knock over a chair and almost fall. Listy turns, a look of pity on her face that somehow makes it all the worse.

"S-sorry..." All my life, love has been a weapon. Feeling it has always been a pretext, a preamble to some kind or other of bloodbath. Thinking of it now *not* as a means to murder feels *wrong…confusing.*

Yet it's *there…a whisper* of that *other* love that Cloister talked about. And the more I feel it, *the more I don't know what to do with it.*

Listy seems to have no such difficulty—unless, of course, she isn't feeling C-Love toward me in the first place. She seems perfectly comfortable in all our interactions, even as I find myself intensely off-balance.

I'm sweating as if I'm in a fight, and my belly's full of butterflies. I wish I'd never come here, opening myself up to all this confusion—even if staying home would have meant certain death without the alliance I'd hoped to find.

Time is running out for that home of mine…though just how quickly, I only now discover.

The door to the deck flies open, and a dark-skinned woman stalks through, heaving for breath. She is a woman I *know,* a messenger from Burytown called Polly Sullivan.

"Sir Gardner!" She gasps out the words. "I bring word of Burytown! Its downfall is *imminent.* This very day, your precious *home* shall fall to the *wolves* at its doorstep."

———

I slide Eros down into his scabbard with the scrape of metal against metal. I do the same for the rest of my blades, slipping them into their various sheaths with familiar, practiced ease.

Standing in the middle of my room, I take a deep breath and release it. Everything is in its place again, and the world makes sense. My course is clear and straight, and my heart is filled with so much *love* for those who threaten my home.

Nodding to myself, I snatch my helmet from a hook on the wall, then storm out of the room and down the stairs. Lord Kendall, Bon Cloister, and Listy wait at the bottom, between me and the exit.

"Ho, sir knight." Rubicon raises both hands as if to hold me back. "We have heard with deep regret the terrible news from Burytown."

"Save your regret for the Loved Ones," I tell him. "For I go now to shower them with my deepest affection."

"Of course," says Rubicon. "You have concluded your business with us in full, then? Shall I signal my man-at-arms to rally the forces we have pledged you?"

I spare a glance at Listy, who bears a troubled look on her face. There is a pull deep within me, a gravity catching at my heart—but other powers overwhelm it.

"Good sir, the people of Burytown shall humbly welcome any and all forces pledged to act in their interest. But it is not true that our business is concluded." I bow my head. "I have yet to fulfill the terms of our pact."

"And *will* you?" asks Rubicon.

I feel Listy's frown upon me as I speak. "If Burytown's state is as dire as Polly Sullivan reports, I cannot promise anything. My own future might be exceedingly brief."

"Then, regrettably, I cannot offer aid," says Rubicon.

"Father!" snaps Listy.

Rubicon slashes his hand through the air. "We risk *much*, sending so large a force away from our own battlements. We risk this very *keep* and all who *depend* on it. We cannot—*will* not—take that risk without a *pact*."

46

"But *I* am the *currency* in this pact, am I not?" says Listy. "Have I *no say* in this…"

Rubicon cuts her off. "The pact is *everything*. In this world, *bargains* are how we *survive*." He shakes his head at Listy, then me. "Let me ask you this, Sir Gardner. Is there *no* possibility of forging a love-that-cherishes between the two of you?"

"I can perform a ceremony here on the spot," says Cloister. "A bond of wedlock so hastily conceived shall be *no* less legitimate."

I look at each of them in turn, considering. Again, when my eyes meet hers, I feel that pull, like the current of a river… but then that *other* force rises up and blots it out. K-Love wins out, as well it should. My people *need* me.

"It is not fair to the people of Burytown to linger one moment more as their home falls to invaders," I say. "And it is not fair to *you* to take your hand in wedlock if I might make of you a widow before this day is done." I bow to Listy. "As much as I might wish it could be otherwise."

"But you are *more* likely to live another day with Lord Kendall's forces at your back," says Cloister.

"And what kind of man would I *be* if I married this woman to save my own *neck*?" Impulsively, I reach for Listy's hand and kiss it. "That does not sound to me like anything *close* to a love-that-cherishes."

I let go of her hand…yet my next words are intended only for *her* ears. "Farewell. Perhaps we shall meet again in that heavenly ocean of mist."

With that, I square my shoulders, push past Lord Kendall, and march outside into the late morning sunlight. Polly, who's been waiting, kickstarts her motorbike and revs it loudly as I don my helmet and climb on behind her.

Then, in a cloud of dust and gravel, we spin around and fly down the highway away from Kendall's Keep.

———

I t surprises me how much I think of Listy as we ride down the mountain. The memory of kissing her hand stays with me, as does the memory of gazing into the mist by her side with her elbow resting against my arm.

But when the time comes to banish her from my thoughts, I do. The field of battle, as I understand all too well, is no place for thoughts of C-Love...only K.

Polly and I dismount and stow the bike a mile back from Burytown, then travel the rest on foot. The sounds of the fight reach us as we hurry through the woods—the clash and clang of steel, the scattered blasts of pistols and rifles, the screams of the wounded and dying.

Then the fight itself reaches us, too. Within sight of the rooftops of town, we are set upon by a trio of Loved Ones, soaked in gore and whipped into a frenzy.

"I *love* you!" A red-bearded warrior leads the ambush, swinging a blood-smeared ax overhead. "I will *show* you *how much!*"

Adrenaline burns in my bloodstream as I slip Eros from his scabbard and stand ready to meet the charge. "*Come* then, brother, and let us *see* who has the *most* love to *give!*"

They attack us like men possessed, half-crazed with K-Love stoked to extreme levels by relentless bloodletting on the field of battle. But Polly and I are possessed by a love that's as strong or stronger and untainted by corrupt motives. Our

48

unwavering brand of love, born of devotion to home and clan, can carry the day against even the longest odds.

Though even as loving as we are, the odds we now face are long indeed. After ending the first three fighters with great love and swordsmanship, Polly and I push closer to the heart of the battle—just in time to see a horde of Loved Ones break through the line of defenders at the edge of Burytown.

People we know go down fighting as the invaders pile on. Every one of our noble warriors smiles with no less loving kindness even as blades, bullets, and war hammers put them to rout.

It is now that I think of Listy once more, for I realize I shall never see her again. With the perimeter breached and our forces so clearly outnumbered, Burytown has not long to live.

Smoke fills the air as flaming arrows set fire to rooftops. Men and women on horseback and motorbikes tear through gaps in the line, escorted by slavering hounds. It is the end of the world, *my* world, and all the smiles and proclamations of love make it all the more hellish.

Doomed as our home may be, Polly and I charge into the fray with smiles and swords flashing.

K-Love, not C-Love. K-Love, not C-Love. Eros swirls and whizzes in my good right hand, slipping through one throat after another. In my good left hand, a dagger jabs and slashes, cutting faces, hearts, and guts like the fang of a dragon.

No mercy is shown, not a whit...though even as my blades sow mayhem, I feel only deep-down love for every soul I maim or kill.

I am, in these moments, perfection—my focus diamond-hard, my killing exquisite, my love unblemished. Dancing from one fighter to the next, leaving geysers of blood in my wake, I am like a holy angel, beaming and unstoppable.

But for every man or woman who falls before me, another three or four or more pile in. For every blow or cut that I deflect, another flurry rains down on me.

I swear I will fight to the last, but the outcome is set in stone now. The end is near.

Polly and I fight back to back, swords and daggers in constant motion—until suddenly, she is gone. Turning in my murderous gyre, I see her dragged under the bloodthirsty tide, and I move to save her.

But at that moment, someone gets in a lucky shot across my back with a crowbar, and I drop. Keeping hold of my blades, I twist, blindly sweeping Eros in a futile swath that catches nothing.

When I hit the ground, the horde closes in around me. *Love you love you love you*, chant dozens of voices overflowing with eager and deeply sincere affection.

I see the crowbar and other bludgeoning weapons hoisted overhead, ready to crash upon me like a landslide. Holding fast to the handles of my blades, I ready myself for one final fusillade to finish the day, one last statement to cast upon the canvas of this terrible work.

"I love you!" I howl the words at the top of my lungs. "*I love you from the bottom of my heart!*"

It is then that I hear a salvo of gunshots crackling nearby. Men topple around me like rotten fruit, dropping their bludgeons.

More clamor then—a thunder of footfalls, a clatter of blades. More gunshots and the twanging of bowstrings, the sizzle and *thunk* of arrows. More men and women fall, and the rest erupt in panic.

Seizing the opportunity, I leap to my feet and pick up where I left off, slashing and stabbing in every direction. As Loved Ones fumble and scatter, I clear them like chaff.

A giant of a man, bald as a pumpkin and bedecked in blood, refuses to panic and swats the helmet right off my head. I answer with a knife through his windpipe...just as a sword thrusts through his heart from behind.

He topples as both blades withdraw—and I see whose sword joined mine in stopping the menace.

It was *hers*. "Good Sir Gardner!" None other than *Listy Kendall* grins back at me from the visor of a white helmet. "Fancy meeting *you* here." Laughing, she wipes the blood from her sword against the hip of her white body armor.

My heart hammers in my chest at the sight of her. I am so caught up in her beauty and the shock of seeing her that I forget to lose the power of speech. "You *came?*" Looking around, I see men and women wearing the coat of arms of Kendall's Keep (in patches or tattoos) plowing through the invaders of Burytown. "But what of the *pact?*"

Listy narrows her eyes and lifts her chin. "Wedded or no, I will *never* stand idly by so long as there is something I can do to save good folk like the people of Burytown."

In that instant, I get a shiver, a frisson of electric joy. I want nothing more than to wrap her in my arms and never let go.

Because she *came*. Because she's *fighting* on behalf of my people for no other reason than because it's *right*. Because she's so *beautiful* and *thoughtful* and *capable* and *confident*, and I *want* her with every fiber of my *being*.

Is *this* what Cloister was talking about? The love-that-cherishes? *An attraction so real and profound that we want to join with the other person in a multitude of ways?*

"I suppose the pact is *moot*, then? Since Burytown got the help it needed without the two of us submitting to wedlock?" As Listy says it, a bruiser roars forth, and she dispatches him with a flick of her sword.

"Actually, I've been thinking." Lifting Listy's visor, I lean in and kiss her gently on the lips. "Perhaps we might discuss *another* pact?"

Her eyes lock with mine, and she kisses me back—not gently. "Perhaps."

Then, whirling, she takes up the fight again, swinging her sword with all the nimble grace with which she paints an ocean of mist on a canvas.

Smiling, I fell an attacker of my own, dropping him dead with a heart full of love—but for *once*, it is *not* the love-that-kills.

IF THE SHOE FITS

DAYLE A. DERMATIS

Dayle A. Dermatis is the author or coauthor of many novels (including snarky urban fantasies Ghosted, Shaded, and Spectered) and more than a hundred short stories in multiple genres appearing in such venues as Fiction River, Alfred Hitchcock's Mystery Magazine, and DAW Books.

In this wonderful story, Dayle takes an old fairy tale and does to it what only Dayle can do. Enjoy.

For a full rundown of all her books, check out www.dayledermatis.com

IF THE SHOE FITS

DAYLE A. DERMATIS

W hen I heard the royal family would be holding a ball to find suitable wife material for the prince and heir, my mind went into overdrive.

But not in the way anyone would expect.

I didn't have specific information about how a royal household was run; I didn't know the number and skill sets of the servants, or even how many people would be invited to this shindig. But within ten minutes I had a pretty good sense of how much it would cost per person, even factoring in peacock meat (which seemed like a waste to me, what with chickens being that much cheaper per pound, but I also understood the art of entertaining sometimes meant being flashy to impress certain guests).

Not, mind you, that it was any of my business. Party planning wasn't really where I wanted to end up, but I loved the idea of it. Just the way my brain works: a challenge, a puzzle. I can put together a fundraising dinner and auction for fifty people without breaking a sweat. The concept of overseeing a royal ball made me go *squee* (on the inside).

Actually going to the ball? Meh. Marrying royalty didn't interest me in the least, and besides, I had finals coming up.

My aunt, Sheila, thought differently.

"It would be a good networking opportunity for you," she'd said.

"I'm not in the market for a husband," I'd said.

She'd rapped my knuckles with her wooden spoon, not enough to hurt, but it got my attention. "Don't be an idiot," she said. "I'm talking about *business* networking. You're about to graduate with honors. All those other girls giggling around the prince? Their daddies will be there, and their daddies run corporations that have job openings for the right candidates."

Oh. Duh. I'd been so busy helping my sisters not lose their freaking minds over the ball that it hadn't even occurred to me that this could be all about the schmoozing. Bad future entrepreneur, no BMW.

There's a reason why Aunt Sheila runs a thriving chain of bakeries.

Around me, young women clumped together, giggling (just as Aunt Sheila had predicted) and craning their necks to get a glimpse of Rupert, Prince Royal and Most Eligible Bachelor. I, on the other hand, had handed out a fair number of business cards, and was feeling rather smug.

Everybody says I work too hard. But I just cannot abide a disorganized house. After my mother died, my father...well, he was grieving, plus he had his own business to run, so the household fell to me. I was still young, but I wasn't stupid. I could clip coupons and plan a week's worth of simple, nutritious meals.

When my dad remarried, bringing not only a new wife into the house but also two new stepsisters for me, I suggested a rota of chores. Seemed only fair. They all laughed and went on gadding about.

So I just went on managing things. Oh, it was a PITA, sure, but with more people in the house, *somebody* had to keep things running smoothly. Money was tight, but I was able to convince dad to let me hire a weekly cleaning lady so I had enough time to work on my degree in business management.

I was thinking about bailing and heading home to get some studying in when the crowd fell silent and parted, and there was Prince Rupert, handsome and dashing. He smiled, white teeth and dimples flashing, and the women around me gave a collective sigh.

Okay, he was a looker, I'll give him that. Piercing blue eyes, thick black hair, square jaw. Broad shoulders, slim hips. Almost a cliché.

He surveyed the people in this corner of the ballroom. I did my best to blend into the wallpaper. It would be the height of rudeness to sneak away, and I had a reputation to cultivate. With all the excitedly heaving bosoms around me, there was no way he'd notice...

Oh, *crap*. He was coming right for me.

He asked me to dance, and women who'd been mentally designing their wedding invitations glared daggers at me as we walked away.

"Your Highness," I said as soon as we were out of earshot of the crowd, "I'm honored by your interest, but I hope you'll allow me to speak plainly."

"Please," he said with a gracious nod of his head that struck me as a little too practiced.

Saying *I'm not interested in you* seemed a little blunt, so I explained that I didn't think I was princess material and that I had plans for a career and I was here largely to put those plans in motion. Only I said it much more politely and flowery.

"Well, I have to thank you for your honesty," he said. "When you first said you weren't princess material, it sounded like a line, but I think you really mean it. Believe me, that's refreshing. I've been desperate to talk to someone who has more on her mind than clinging to my every word and answering in a charming way that's designed to make me think she's The One."

It was quite a speech, let me tell you.

"If you want to find a potential wife tonight, you probably ought to be dancing with them, not me," I said.

"Protocol states I must give you the full dance," he said, "and I appreciate the chance to talk to someone interesting. Plus, I've been dying to ask you: where did you get your shoes?"

My...huh? What?

Aunt Sheila had loaned them to me. She'd studied in Paris back in the day, and saved up her money for the one indulgence. I didn't know a shoe from a ship, but I knew these were exquisite, so-expensive-it-takes-your-breath-away pumps. They were, I knew, one of a kind, too—the burgundy silk and black lace were remnants, and no other pair had been made with the same fabrics.

I explained it all to Rupert (who was, I might mention, an incredibly good dancer).

"They really are fabulous," he said. "I wish I could get a better look at them. Would you like a drink?"

I blinked, recovered, and the next thing I knew we were in

a private antechamber and I was drinking the best damn champagne on earth and he was turning one of my shoes over in his hands and examining the workmanship. He seemed to know what he was looking at.

He handed the pump back to me (I'd been afraid he'd gently replace it on my foot or something) and I slipped it on.

"You're so lucky," he said.

"Why?" I couldn't quite get that. He had the world at his fingertips, didn't he?

"You have choices," he said, "and the freedom to make those choices. My path is set: marry a suitable woman, produce heirs, be the figurehead for a kingdom that already has a perfectly well-running government. The end."

Well...I'd never thought about that. "But there's so much you can do, with your connections and power. What about creating charities?"

"My future wife is expected to do that," he said. "Don't get me wrong, though—I do see those benefits. It's just that I'd give anything to have the freedom to pursue my own passions, live my own life." He waved a hand. "Oh, never mind."

I wanted to tell him to just go do whatever he bloody well wanted, because really, who was really going to protest? Wasn't his decree practically law?

Then I thought about it. I could very well have moved out and left the chaos of my family home behind me, giving me tons more time to move ahead with my own plans. But I felt a responsibility to them—just as Rupert must feel toward the kingdom.

So we talked about that, and I have to say, he was pretty

IF THE SHOE FITS

easy to talk to. I kinda liked him, in a "I've never had a brother" sort of way.

His counselor peeking in the door made us both realize how long ago we'd ditched the ball, and made me realize just how late it was.

Crap.

There'd been no way in hell I could have driven there; the traffic was beyond a gridlocked nightmare. There wouldn't be any cabs. So if I didn't catch the last train, which left Palace Station just after midnight, I'd be stranded.

"Reallynicetalkingtoyou, gottago."

I grabbed my stuff from the coat check, laced on my sneakers (there was no way in hell I was going to commute in those stilettos, either), and made a mad dash to the train station.

It was only after I was sitting in the car and catching my breath that I realized I'd dropped one of the shoes somewhere along the way.

I said a word that *never* would have been appropriate in front of royalty.

———

Thankfully Aunt Sheila was out of town, so I didn't have to break the loss to her just yet. I was eyeballs-deep in finals over the next few days, pulling all-nighters at the library and crashing on a friend's sofa closer to the university, so I didn't hear about the whole ruckus until I stumbled home.

"Where have you been; I've left messages," my stepmom said.

I pulled out my cell. Yep, there were messages. Who knew?

"The palace has been looking for you." She twisted her hands together. "We were hoping they were calling about Genna or Clara."

"It's just about my shoe," I said. "I dropped it when I was leaving. I'm sure they just want to return it."

But even I wondered why they couldn't have just popped it into the mail, you know?

So I called back, and was put on hold forever (royal Muzak is no better than your local bank's, believe me) before someone got back on the line and told me that Prince Rupert would like to return the shoe to me personally and was I free for a private dinner at the palace tomorrow?

That just didn't bode well. I'd caught up on the news and knew that the prince hadn't selected a prospective wife (or even a short list of candidates) since the ball. I couldn't imagine Rupert taking the time to hang out with me when he had bigger fish to fry…unless it was my fish he had an interest in.

Had I not made myself clear? Had *he* not made himself clear?

But I had to get that shoe back before Aunt Sheila got home.

I had a private audience with the prince in the "small" dining room, which was almost the size of my father's house. At least we weren't at opposite ends of the table that yawned the length of the room. If we had, we'd've needed walkie-talkies.

We made small talk through the soup course, and then he leaned forward and said, "Ella."

His tone of voice made me vaguely itchy. I doubted I'd like what he had to say. "Your Highness."

"I have a business proposition for you."

Oh. Well, then. I sat forward. "I'm always interested in that."

"I need a wife."

I sat back. "I don't—"

"Please, hear me out." He looked almost as unhappy as I felt, so I let him continue. "I've met many fine women, so many who would be appropriate for the role of princess. But I have some...special requirements, and I don't believe any of those women would understand or agree to them."

Great. He had a kinky streak.

"Those women are looking for a great romance, and that's something I can never give them," he continued.

Oh. A mistress, then, someone he could never put on the throne.

But no. He kept going. "You have other goals in life, ones that I can facilitate. I think we can both benefit from a joint venture."

He went on to detail what I'd get out of the deal, which included some pretty nifty corporate responsibilities. In return, I'd be his wife essentially in name only, and he'd be able to pursue his personal passions, as he'd called them.

The prenup included a confidentiality agreement, and when I read it, it was like a blinding light going off over my head. All of the signs had been there, but like everyone else, I just hadn't put them together.

His disinterest in the sea of heaving bosoms. His fascination with my fabulous shoes...

———

S o there you have it. Rupert remains the country's figurehead, and designs shoes and handbags (and occasionally hats) under a fake name. He's quite good; his latest line got a huge write-up in *Vogue*. We pay a private physician handsomely to keep quiet about the artificial insemination to get me pregnant. (Yeah, I've always focused on getting a career, but I never said kids were out of the question.)

And me? I get to be CFO of Rupert's design firm *and* manage the royal finances, and for fun I throw elaborate, glittering dinner parties and fundraisers for up to a thousand people.

Squee.

UP ON THE ROOFTOP

KRISTINE GRAYSON

Kristine Kathryn Rusch is a New York Times *and* USA Today *bestselling writer and maybe the most award-winning and prolific writer working today. She has won more awards in science fiction and mystery than just about anyone alive and she is the only person to win the Hugo Award for her writing as well as her editing.*

She writes under three major names, Kristine Kathryn Rusch, Kris Nelscott, and Kristine Grayson. Plus a few minor names. This fantastic holiday novella is under the Grayson name and has a lot of elements of her holiday world that she has written other Grayson stories and novels in. They are all super fun.

You can find out a lot more about Kris's work at her publisher, WMG Publishing Inc. www.wmgpublishinginc.com or her website www.kriswrites.com

UP ON THE ROOFTOP

KRISTINE GRAYSON

Julka stood on the roof, hands on her hips, feet covered in snow. She was tired, she was cold, and she hadn't felt the tip of her nose in hours. She was staring at yet another fancy-pants chimney, a narrow little pipe sticking up out of a lovely square pile of fake bricks, and she wanted to kick it.

Which wasn't very festive of her.

But seriously, who felt festive on October 30th? It was New England, for heavens sake. There wasn't supposed to be snow for another—oh, what? Two weeks? She really didn't know, except that she had checked the records going back to the 19th century, and never found a snowfall as deep as this one before Halloween. She wasn't supposed to be this cold for another month, and by then, she should've been moving south. Where she would have to deal with freezing fog, sleet, and sheets of ice.

Oh, joy. Ho-ho-ho and all that.

It was her own damn fault that she was standing here. She

was the one who had said, I don't have the skills to run a workshop, but I can find problems and solve them.

And then, of course, she had to go too far, because she always went too far: Besides, I don't want to stay here for my entire life. I'd like to travel. I need to see the world. I really, really do.

She sighed. When she had said she wanted to see the world, she had hoped she would be placed in one of the many year-round outposts. She would receive toy shipments, interview local children, and make certain that the back-up sleighs were in fantastic shape. She would scout local products and find great toy factories that didn't even know they would be enlisted.

She had wanted to be one of the Ambassadors for Santa's massive worldwide operation.

She hadn't meant that she wanted to be a minion in Entry Access Quality Control, someone who had to view each and every house with children in it for the appropriate entrance. Appropriate, in Santa's rather medieval mind, always meant a chimney.

She sighed and clutched the tablet to her chest. It was a real paper tablet—one of the millions of Big Chief tablets that someone in Santa's North Pole headquarters had stocked up on in the 1960s, along with stubby Number 2 pencils that she refused to use.

She wanted an electronic tablet—a gizmo, with bells and whistles and access to the worldwide web (even though, she'd been told, no one called it that any more). The workshop had hundreds of those as well, but not for the elves or the human support staff, but for the tech-savvy children who didn't want a dolly or a train set, but who wanted the latest in computer gadgetry.

Everyone at the North Pole had to be careful with gadgetry. Many types of magic—particularly fairy tale magic—weren't compatible with electronics. Elven magic also had difficulty with electronics. Santa always had the Fairy Kingdoms design his systems, and that didn't always work well.

Delbert popped his head out of the invisible sleigh. She hated the effect. It made him look like he'd been beheaded, and she had gotten stuck with the head part. She wondered what the civilians on the ground saw. Whatever it was, it couldn't've been pretty.

Entry Access Quality Control wasn't supposed to call attention to itself. That was why the invisible sleigh, which was the same size and shape as Santa's (only without the reindeer; they hadn't needed reindeer since 1930 or so, but they kept the reindeer for form's sake. Besides, the reindeer had a hell of a union).

Delbert usually remained invisible as well. He was an S-Elf, sharing a lineage with Santa. Delbert hated his heritage, and would've fled long ago except that he couldn't hide who he was, no matter how much he wanted to. All those photos of Santa vacationing on the beach, of Santa in Hawaii in the summer or lounging in Monte Carlo instead of driving his sleigh—well, they weren't Santa.

They were usually Delbert.

And as punishment for tarnishing the Santa brand, he had to spend one year on Entry Access Quality Control.

"Well," Delbert said, "do I have to put my boots on?"

"No," Julka said sourly. He might have been punished by doing Entry Access Quality Control, but she was the one who suffered. She inspected, kicked, shook, and fought with more chimneys than she wanted to consider. Yes, she had the best boots and gloves that magic could conjure, but she still got cold and wet and grumpy.

Delbert only had to emerge when there was a likely chimney, which there hadn't been all day.

The rules of Entry Access Quality Control were pretty simple: if the chimney didn't work, and the skylight looked too dicey, then Santa got to use any available door. And Delbert didn't have to check the doors. With the growing obesity problem worldwide, the entire slew of Santa Advance Teams no longer had to worry about doorways being too narrow for the Jolly Old Elf.

"I'll boil up some lunch then," Delbert said. "You gonna want any?"

"No, thanks." She couldn't stomach a second day of Peppermint Veal Stew, even if the elves did think it a delicacy. Her stomach didn't. Neither did her taste buds. That was the other problem of traveling with elves. They preferred sweet foods to almost everything else, turning the most disgusting things into candy.

She'd grown up with it, but that didn't mean she liked it. After the last few days, she deserved something made here in the Greater World, not that it was greater than the North Pole's magical universe. The Greater World was just bigger—and lacked the magic.

Which she was really beginning to appreciate.

Because magic—what little of it she had—was making her cold.

———

M arshall Collier shaded his eyes with his right hand, and looked up at the roof. It wasn't a trick of the light. He was seeing a slight figure holding some kind of notebook kick a chimney. Tiny runnels of snow trickled down the side of the rooftop, like the precursors of an avalanche.

Or at least, a severe loss of roof-snow that would ruin the shoveling work he had managed earlier this morning.

Marshall had a narrow flatbed truck that could hold a small Caterpillar tractor with a large shovel on the end, and two different size snow blowers. He also had real honest-to-God shovels tucked into the back and three changes of clothing, including pairs of boots.

He'd been out clearing side streets and sidewalks since 5 a.m, calling the power company every two blocks or so to report downed lines, and doing his best to be a Good Samaritan.

This freak pre-Halloween blizzard, and his parka, had given him a kind of anonymity that he hadn't had since the Great Recession began. It hadn't mattered that he hadn't worked for the fraudulent companies that caused the meltdown. What mattered was that he had made a lot of money (too much money) as an investment banker and venture capitalist. It also didn't matter that he had retired from that business in 2007 at the age of 34. What seemed to matter to all these folks who were struggling to pay their now-overpriced mortgages on their meager unemployment benefits, was that he had once worked in that industry, and that meant he was one step above Satan.

And maybe he was. When he worked in the industry, he hadn't thought that there were actual people behind the numbers. He wasn't a sales guy. He had been an analysis guy. He hadn't dealt with people; he had dealt with numbers.

As the economy tumbled into darker and darker places, he had watched the news reports with horror, realizing that each number he had played with had represented someone else's money.

The thing was, he hadn't been told that when he was hired straight out of Harvard. No one said a word as he had manipulated the numbers, stroked and fondled them and made them grow—legitimately—until the returns he got weren't good enough for his bosses. They wanted him to cheat on the math. He never cheated on anything. Not on tests, not on girlfriends, and certainly not on something as important as his job.

So he got fired for not taking enough risks. But he had already taken a big risk: he had put some of his earnings into a buddy's company. The company looked dicey from the beginning, but a friend was a friend, right? He had then invested in a few other companies, calling himself a venture capitalist, when really he was a depressed fired former investment banker.

And then his buddy's company became a huge success. And Marshall, as one of the early investors, made a fortune.

He pulled out of the venture capital business because he didn't want to make his fortune into an obscene fortune, especially not while his neighbors were starving. So he concentrated his efforts on helping charities become more efficient—manipulating numbers again, but for a good cause. (And giving away money.)

But he never talked about any of that, and everyone in this rather toney neighborhood thought of him as that investment banker guy. Hated, as if he had robbed all those funds all by himself.

He had no idea why he kept trying to ingratiate himself with the people in this place, but he did. He kept telling himself it was because he liked his house and he didn't want to move—which was true—but honestly, it might've been because he was trying to ingratiate himself with himself. He had let himself become part of the problem, and he really hadn't tried to implement a solution, back when there could have been one.

Guilt. It went a long way. Including getting him out at 5 a.m. on a blizzardy morning, clearing roads and driveways for people who would spit on him if they knew he was the one behind the wheel of the snow blower.

Still, six hours of work later, he was feeling pretty good. He wasn't cold, he wasn't wet, and he had managed to clear miles of roadway and driveway with by his own rather mighty self.

Sometimes good physical labor felt a lot better than massaging numbers. Even if that meant he was seeing the same people over and over again on rooftops.

Although that wasn't really accurate. He was seeing the same person over and over again on rooftops. She was tiny, slender, and stylish, wearing a little red cape with fur trim. (He hoped it was fake fur trim. In this neighborhood, wearing fur could get her killed.) She also had on reddish pants tucked into knee-high boots. She was wearing fur earmuffs and no gloves at all. And she looked cold.

When he had first seen her, he thought she was a child. She was so slim and so regal, and her outfit so outlandish for someone going from roof to roof, that he figured she had to be about twelve. A few houses ago, he had gotten closer, and realized if she was twelve, she should've been locked inside the house.

She had a curvy figure appropriate to her small size, and golden blond hair that he hadn't seen outside of shampoo commercials. He couldn't quite see her face, but her body language wasn't twelve either. It was exasperated adult—or it had been, until she gave the chimney in front of her one frustrated kick.

He frowned at her. He had no idea why a woman dressed like she was heading for a Macy's Christmas photo shoot would travel from rooftop to rooftop in a MacMansion-filled Connecticut neighborhood. Nor did he know exactly how she was doing it. Or what angered her about it so much.

He did know that he found her fascinating, from the tip of her golden hair to her impractical boots. He wondered if he should yell up at her and warn her that too many sudden movements would cause the snow to slide off the roof—and her with it.

Then she stomped away from him, toward the back of the house. She reached the peak of the roof, stepped up some kind of ladder that he couldn't see—and vanished.

And not a wink-out disappear complete with little sparklies. Nor was it like a transporter vanish in Star Trek where the entire body fuzzed into a multicolored light show. It was as if she got swallowed by something. First her head and shoulders disappeared, along with one of her feet and an arm, then her torso, and finally the remaining foot. All that remained was a disturbance in the Force (as Obi-Wan would have said), which looked rather like a heat mirage, floating briefly next to that chimney.

Then nothing. Nothing at all. Not even the house next door. At least, not for a few seconds, anyway. It was as if someone had set up an opaque wall, designed to match the snow and the gray cloud cover (which was threatening even more ugliness).

He blinked and the neighbor's rooftop reappeared. And so did a few more rooftops he hadn't known were missing.

Okay, that was it. Six hours of physical labor in the cold, moving tractors and snow blowers and piles of snow, subsisting on stale (lukewarm) coffee, breakfast bars, and one apple, had not done him any good.

It was time to take a break. It was past time to take a break.

He sighed, rubbed his eyes, and headed to lunch.

———

It had taken Julka fifteen minutes to convince Delbert that she needed to stop at the Burger King two miles away. He just wanted to go to the next rooftop. He had some vision of getting done before nightfall. Like that was going to happen. They wouldn't be done until the morning of December 23rd. Although to be fair, he was only referring to this town, and in this town they only had 35 houses left to go.

Besides, they had already earned hotel money. Julka liked that best of all. The teams that couldn't get their quotas done in the time allotted had to sleep in their sleighs. But Julka and Delbert were one day ahead of schedule, partly because of the blizzard. They'd worked around it, using the North Pole Navigator to let them know when and where the worst of the weather would be. Then they would go to the safest part of their region, get the work done, and move onto another area, avoiding most of the snow the entire time.

The Burger King's roof had been shoveled off. It had a single pipe that spewed smoke that smelled of frying beef. A gigantic Halloween pumpkin balloon had been shredded by the blizzard's middle-of-the-night winds and hung off the roof like orange streamers. Since reddish orange was one of Burger King's primary colors, the streamers looked planned.

Nothing else did. The parking lot was jammed. Julka had to convince Delbert to land on the nearby health club's roof. She had hoped to land in the parking lot.

But the parking lot—which was huge—was also full.

She sat on the roof's edge, feet crossed, watching as locals streamed into that Burger King. Rules dictated that she wait until no one was around, so that she wouldn't be seen, which was one reason why she chose the health club's roof. But if she waited much longer, she'd eat shingles.

A guy with a huge rig filled with all kinds of snow-moving equipment parked in the auxiliary parking lot, as far from anyone as he could get. He climbed out of his four-by-four, pushed the hood of a parka off his head, and wiped his face.

He had beautiful black hair in need of a trim. He was tall and broad-shouldered, and moved with the ease of an athlete. He didn't look up as he walked, and she felt oddly disappointed. She wanted to see his face.

She had a feeling she'd seen him before, but she had no idea where.

She lost sight of him in the scrum of vehicles in the main parking lot. He had been the last non-magical person in her line of vision. She grinned, then launched herself off the roof.

Jumping from rooftops had not been one of her magical

skills until she took this job. Then she got an augmentation just so she was protected from accidental slippage or falls of more than three feet. This was the best perk of all—that feeling of floating through a cushion of air. It made her feel like she could fly if she would only put her mind to it.

She landed on the sidewalk outside the health club. She adjusted her hair and her ear muffs, hoping she looked enough like a regular person—a regular American person—to get by.

This was the one thing she had little experience with, the one thing she valued the most: the opportunity to mingle with regular people, the kind the Pole was designed to help. She knew she could never quite blend in, but she could at least experience everything like the tourist she was, making memories, snatching moments out of other people's every day lives and wondering what she would have been like if she had been born in New England instead of the North Pole.

She squared her shoulders, adjusted her cape, and headed for the front door.

———

Normally, Marshall was a "my-body-is-my-temple" kinda guy. He watched what he ate, exercised regularly, and got enough sleep. After six hours of intensive labor in the frigid cold, he figured it wasn't going to hurt him to eat poorly.

And he was planning to eat very poorly.

He pulled into Burger King like it was the holy of holies. He looked at that cheesy sign he usually drove past (with his head down so he didn't have to contemplate all that burgery goodness) and reveled in the idea of a Whopper or a bacon-double cheeseburger or maybe both, along with fifteen sides of fries, and eighteen regular Cokes.

He'd spend his afternoon in the plastic seats, leaning against a faux marble table, and watching the neighborhood go by. His neighbors would shun him and treat him badly and he would have to hide behind the pieces of The New York Times someone had carelessly left lying about.

That thought—and not the fifteen orders of fries—nearly had him swerving for the drive-through.

But he hadn't. He had forced himself to go inside.

He had never seen the Burger King so busy. People lined up five deep. Entire families huddled together, looking miserable. It wasn't until he eavesdropped that he understood why.

Many houses in the neighborhood had no power. Burger King was the closest fast-food restaurant—any restaurant, really—with electricity. A woman behind the counter grinned tiredly at one customer, and said, "We've been like this all morning."

Startled, Marshall looked at the clock. It was morning to most people. His day was half done. More than half done, really. And now that he had stopped moving, he was done in.

No wonder he'd been seeing pretty girl elves on rooftops. He was half asleep on his feet.

He ordered a Double Whopper with large fries and both Coke and coffee—the coffee for warmth.

Lucky him, he found an open table that fit two, so he didn't feel like he was taking spots away from cold families. Everyone sounded miserable. Kids asking if they could trick or treat when the power was out; parents giving the time-honored "we'll see" response that probably meant no. If power lines were still down, then no one was wandering neighborhoods in costume any time soon, and he doubted that anyone would have the time or the ability to set up a one-stop trick-or-treat place.

He'd never seen anything quite like it: this full blizzard so early in the season, wrecking so many plans.

"I'd blame you for this, except I, at least, know you're not God," said one of his neighbors, Hester Bain, as she walked by Marshall with her ten-year-old son, Nigel.

Nigel gave Marshall an apologetic glance. Marshall shrugged. Hester Bain ("That's Mrs. Bain to you") had been vicious to him from the moment she found out who he had been, at a neighborhood meeting from late 2008 that he still regretted—not that he went to the meeting, but that he had said, "I know a lot of those guys—I used to work in the industry—and believe me, most of them don't have souls."

Apparently "most of them" had applied to him too. He tried to shrug moments like this off—after all, the Bains had lost all of their life savings with one of the scam investment houses, and they had barely managed to hang onto their house —but the words still hurt.

He made himself look away from her. He didn't want to meet anyone's gaze. He didn't want to provoke more comments.

Then a flash of red caught his eye. He turned toward the door, and his breath caught.

There she was: taller than he had initially thought, older too—maybe 30—with a face as stunning as her wheat-blond hair. High cheekbones, blue eyes, delicate lips—she looked like a Russian supermodel.

She also looked stunningly out of place. It wasn't just her

red cape with the fur trim and matching red pants tucked into those black leather boots. It was the happy expression on her face.

Everyone else was miserable, a bit frightened, worried about the weather and the future, and she smiled like she had entered the happiest place on Earth.

Plus it was the day before Halloween, and she looked like Santa's Naughty Helper before the half-naked photo shoot started.

His cheeks warmed, and he forced himself to look away. He normally didn't think of women like that, not even exceedingly pretty women. Not even exceedingly pretty women whom he found exceedingly attractive.

He could feel her nearby. He wondered if she was staring at him, then decided that he was just being silly. She hadn't noticed him at all. In fact, if she was from the neighborhood, she probably knew what an awful person he was supposed to be and would most certainly avoid him.

At least she hadn't been a figment of his imagination. Although that begged the question—what had she been doing on that rooftop?

Those rooftops, if he really wanted to be accurate.

He wanted to get up and ask her. He wondered how creepy that would be. Would she think he was spying on her or something?

"Pardon me," a low female voice with an odd accent asked him.

He lifted his head, and there she was, large as life and much more fragrant. She smelled peppermint, which somehow didn't surprise him one bit.

"Is this seat taken?" she asked softly. "It seems to be the only one available."

"Um, sure," he said. "I mean, no. I mean, please, sit down."

When was the last time a woman had him tongue-tied? When was the last time he had spoken to an attractive woman? He broke up with his most recent girlfriend a year ago, he didn't go to bars to meet women, and no one in town wanted anything to do with him. He would have had to take a train into New York City just to find a woman who didn't mind his background.

The pretty woman smiled at him, and the entire room brightened. He was surprised that no one else seemed to notice.

"Thank you," she said and slipped into the hard plastic chair, setting her tray down as she did. "I have wanted to come here for a long time."

To Connecticut? To Burger King? To this Burger King? He knew she hadn't meant the table or the spot near the window.

"I take it you're not local," he said, and silently cursed himself for being idiotic.

"Sadly, no," she said. "I am only in your fair city for a few days for work. Then I move south."

"Move south?" he asked.

She shrugged one shoulder. "My work requires that I go from place to place."

"And your work is on...rooftops?" he asked.

She looked at him, surprised. "How do you know that?"

"I saw you today," he said. "It's hard to miss you in that red cape."

She looked down at herself as if she just realized what she was wearing. "Is it inappropriate?"

"I don't know," he said. "It is the day before Halloween. But usually people reserve their elf costumes for Christmas."

"Elf costume?" she said in a decidedly frigid tone.

"Well, you know," Marshall said, his cheeks getting even warmer. "The red cape, the fur, the boots..."

God, he almost blurted that she looked like Santa's Naughty Helper, but he somehow managed to censor that statement. Still, she looked offended.

"I am not an elf," she said.

"I-I-I know," he said. "I'm sorry. I didn't mean to insult you. It's a very fetching costume."

He sounded so lame, like some needy geek around a pretty girl. Which he was. Before he had gotten into Harvard, hell, before he had become an investment banker, long before he had money, he had been the math geek in the corner of the high school cafeteria, lost in his numbers, unable to talk to any girl he found attractive—even if (especially if) she had asked him about her math homework.

"It's not a costume," she said in that same frosty tone. "It's my work outfit."

His face probably matched her suit. He didn't even know how to apologize without making things worse.

"Ah," he said. "It's just unusual to see people in red uniforms standing on rooftops in the lull of a snowstorm."

"Oh," she said, "the storm is over—at least here. It's moving north and east."

She sounded so sure of herself.

"That's not what the weather people say." Marshall had checked his phone twice to see the weather, wondering if his labors this morning had even been worthwhile. The weather experts seemed to believe the blizzard would continue—in one form or another—until November.

"Well, we have much more sophisticated equipment," she said.

"We?" he asked.

She shrugged. "The people I work with. We have fantastic equipment, especially about the weather. We have to."

Because they spent their days on rooftops? He felt confused. "I suppose I can't ask who you work with."

She shook her head. Her sandwich was almost gone, and he hadn't even noticed her eating it. "You wouldn't believe me if I told you."

He flashed on that face he had seen on one of the rooftops —the first one?—the face that looked like a disembodied head. Was that one of her partners? Or was that a trick of the light?

He was about to ask her, when a strident female voice cut into their conversation. "I don't know who you are, young lady, but you look nice."

Marshall and the pretty non-elf woman looked toward the sound. It came from Mrs. Bain, two tables away, her lunch crumpled in front of her, her tray pushed to one side. Nigel had his head down, trying to finish his Whopper Jr.

Mrs. Bain leaned toward them as if she was going to speak confidentially, but she didn't lower her voice at all.

"But," Mrs. Bain continued, "that man is one of those bankers who steals from people. He's not the sort of person you should idly converse with. He's despicable."

"What?" The pretty non-elf woman frowned at Mrs. Bain, then looked at Marshall. "Do you mean him?"

He almost closed his eyes. He didn't want to see the disappointment on her face.

But she didn't look disappointed. Just confused.

"I don't understand all the customs here," she was saying, "but why would a banker have snow removal equipment on the back of a big truck?"

Marshall's breath caught. She had seen that? She had been watching him too?

"He probably repossessed it," Mrs. Bain said with great certainty. "It would be just his style to repossess the equipment when people need it most."

"Mom." Nigel touched his mother's arm. "He's been digging people out all day. That's how we got out of our driveway."

Mrs. Bain gave Nigel an alarmed look. "You let him on our property? You were supposed to shovel."

Nigel bowed his head and grabbed some French fries as if they would save him. His face was as red as Marshall's had been.

"To be fair, Mrs. Bain," Marshall said, "there was too much snow for anyone to handle with a shovel."

"Fair?" she snapped. "Don't you talk to me about fair. Don't you talk to any of us about fair."

Marshall sighed. He knew better. He shouldn't have engaged. He never should have said anything. And now the pretty non-elf woman probably thought he was some kind of monster on top of being a clueless tongue-tied idiot.

"Mom," Nigel said softly, without looking up. His fries were arranged in a neat row on his tray. "You're not being nice."

Mrs. Bain stood, then grabbed her empty tray, and Nigel's half-full one. "Someday, Nigel, you'll learn that there are people in this world who don't deserve nice."

Marshall would have had to agree with that, but only because he was angry, and he didn't dare say anything. Why had she butted into his life? Why did she want to ruin it?

Oh, yeah, because people like him had ruined hers—and his was the face of the disaster, at least to her. He had to keep reminding himself of that.

"Where I work," the pretty non-elf woman said, "we believe all can be redeemed, if they realize they've been naughty."

It took Marshall a moment to understand what she had said. First, he had heard the word "naughty," and that had conjured the wrong image for him. He didn't need to hear her say the word "naughty," not after he had thought it—twice.

But he got past that (he hoped) and realized that the pretty non-elf woman was defending him. It was such an unusual experience that he didn't know what to say.

"Lie to yourself all you like, honey," Mrs. Bain said. "A man like that will disillusion you fast enough. Come along, Nigel."

Nigel shot Marshall another apologetic look. Marshall nodded as imperceptively as he could, and watched as the two of them stalked off. Well, as Mrs. Bain stalked. Nigel trailed like a lost puppy.

"What did you do to them?" the pretty non-elf woman asked.

So much for defense. Guilty until proven innocent. Actually, guilt by association. Years of association, actually.

He had no idea how to explain any of it, especially to a woman who clearly wasn't from around here. She had been kind. She didn't need to hear about his strange existence.

"It's a long story," he said.

"Well," she said. "I've got some time. I'm ahead of schedule, and now that I'm done with this Whopper thing, I'm going to try something else."

Then she grinned, got up, and headed back to the counter.

He watched her in surprise. He had no idea where she was going to put another entire meal—and he shouldn't be watching her, not like this, not with the word "naughty" still floating around in his brain.

He should do the honorable thing: He should get up and leave. Right now. That way he wouldn't embarrass himself any more and he wouldn't upset the neighbors.

But this was the nicest anyone had been to him in a long time—at least, anyone local.

Only she wasn't local.

And somehow, the job she did had something to do with being nice.

So maybe "nice" was just a reflex for her. Still, it made him feel better. He hadn't realized how down he had been until the pretty non-elf woman stood up for him.

He sipped his now-cold coffee. Then he realized that the Burger King was quiet. Most of the patrons were staring at him. Most of them recognized him, either from the neighborhood or those ill-advised neighborhood meetings.

If the pretty non-elf woman stayed here for a few days, she would want a good experience. And people wouldn't be nice to her if they thought she was a friend of his.

He put the lid on his coffee so that he wouldn't spill it, and stood up. He needed to leave. Not for him so much, but for her. She didn't need to get sucked into his world, not even for an hour, not in a fast-food restaurant where half the neighborhood had gone for lunch. She had looked so joyful when she had come in here.

He didn't want—even inadvertently—to trample on that joy.

———

H e was cute. No, he was better than cute. He was nice. And really handsome with that dark hair (which needed just a bit of a trim), a little stubble from his long day, and the redness in his cheeks. She hadn't seen a man with such redness in his cheeks this far from home, and she found that she liked it.

Julka stood at the end of the line, bouncing a little on her feet. She liked him, even if other people didn't seem to. He seemed kind. She had no idea what he had done to that horrible lady. (Then Julka sighed at herself: she wasn't supposed to think of anyone as horrible, just unreformed.) And even though he had supposedly treated that lady poorly, he had shoveled her walk, saving her little boy from doing work that might have hurt him.

Because the handsome man was right: anyone with snow experience knew that too much snow had fallen in a short period of time to get rid of it with a simple shovel. It would take mechanical equipment (for the non-magical humans) or some real magical muscle to get rid of the snow in a timely fashion.

89

And as she had learned throughout her long years at the North Pole, some snow simply refused to be gotten rid of.

She made herself look at the menu. So many choices. If she had known that there were this many choices in all of the various restaurants in the Greater World, she would have stopped eating Delbert's cooking long ago. She had Greater World money, with more of it appearing as she completed each day's task.

Julka turned toward the table only to see the handsome man get up. His shoulders were hunched forward and he was holding his tray in his left hand. He looked defeated.

Something in that interaction with the horrible woman (to heck with it: that appellation was staying) had really bothered him.

"Don't go," she said, slipping out of her place in line. "I'll buy you a fresh coffee."

He gave her that sad smile of his and shook his head. He came toward her, and said softly, "Look, I'm not the most popular person here, and talking to me might ruin your time in this town. So it's best if we don't—"

"Nonsense," she said. "They already saw us talking. Whatever damage there was is done. Besides, I have some things to ask you."

His sad smile got sadder.

"No," he said. "It's best if we just part ways now. But thank you for your kindness. It means a lot to me."

Then he bowed his head, and walked out of the Burger King.

She almost hurried after him—she hated seeing anyone that upset—but he had been clear. He didn't think it was good for her to be talking to him.

Which just showed his kindness again.

After he disappeared from view, she rejoined the line. Everyone was staring at her—except for the people who were studiously avoiding her gaze. No one was talking.

"What did he do?" she asked the silver-haired man in the table next to her.

"I'm not sure," the man said, his tone dismissive.

But she wasn't going to let it go. "What do you mean, you're not sure. Everyone is treating him like he's done something awful."

"Well, he did," the man said. "We're just not sure what."

"He was an investment banker," said the little old lady at the table across from the man, her tones hushed as if she had called the gentleman Julka had been talking to a sex crimes pervert.

"Isn't that a common job?" Julka asked.

"Not exactly," the woman said. "And he is retired."

"So what is the problem?" Julka asked.

"Well, those bankers," the woman said, "they caused the meltdown."

Meltdown? Oh, the woman meant that financial thing that happened a few years back. Julka had to study it in Advanced Greater World Studies, so that she could converse about it. The "meltdown" had a serious impact on children worldwide, making Santa's services even more necessary, and overwhelmed him with extra work.

"You think he had something to do with that?" Julka asked, referring to her handsome gentleman. How could he have? He seemed so nice.

"They all did, those bankers," the woman said in hushed tones.

"And some of 'em really screwed people," the silver-haired man said. "They took money from everyone, leaving us with nothing."

Julka looked out the door, as if she could still see the gentleman. "So why was he digging people out?"

"He seems to think we'll accept him as a neighbor," another woman said snidely from the back. "But we never will. Him and his ilk, they ruined us."

A bunch of others nodded.

"Can't you forgive him?" Julka asked.

Everyone stared at her as if she had grown a third head.

She shrugged. "I mean, he seems really sorry."

"There are some things in life," said the silver-haired man, "that sorry doesn't solve."

———

M arshall was cold, wet, tired and discouraged. He had promised himself that he wouldn't quit until he'd finished the last of the neighborhood, but as he drove down the one plowed street, he saw orange wooden saw horses on the road, with a hand-made sign that warned of more downed power lines.

Earlier in the day, he would have figured out a way around so that he could finish his self-assigned mission, but this time, he simply didn't want to go on. He wanted to get home, take a warm shower, and forget that the day ever happened.

Part of the problem with his neighbors was his house. It was too big for the neighborhood. It didn't matter that he hadn't built it: he had bought it, back when he was feeling flush—a large Tudor/Colonial blend that actually worked. It sat on a rise overlooking the entire neighborhood, and underneath the house proper was a gigantic garage that originally housed the first owner's antique car collection.

As Marshall rounded the corner, he hit the garage door opener, then wished he hadn't. The driveway was snowed in again. He had cleared it at five a.m., but there had been quite a bit of snow since then, and even more had toppled off the hillside. The garage door was open, but there was no driving inside until he cleared a path.

He pulled into the turn-around in front of the driveway, shut off the engine and rested his head on the steering wheel. He was inclined to chain the equipment to the truck with padlocks and go inside.

But he knew better. Given the way the neighborhood felt about him, someone would damage the equipment, and he would just blame himself for leaving it outside.

He sighed. Today proved one thing. It didn't matter how much he did, how hard he tried or how many times he explained that he had retired before the collapse. He would always be a pariah here.

Much as he loved his house—and he really did—he would have to move. He couldn't stay. He needed to find some other nifty house in another nifty neighborhood—and then he had to avoid the neighborhood meetings, or if he went, he would simply say that he was a retired numbers runner. Because, in essence, that was all he had done.

He had run numbers for a bunch of gamblers who had ignored him anyway. They were getting off scott-free, and he was staying here, inadvertently paying for their mistakes.

And missing opportunities with pretty women who wore inappropriate elf costumes at the end of October, women (woman) who had the most enchanting accent and the loveliest blue eyes he had ever seen.

Too bad he had met her under such strange circumstances.

Too bad he would never see her again.

He certainly would have loved to find out exactly who she was.

———

S he shouldn't have let him go. Julka slipped out of the line, and headed for the door. The poor man. Everyone in this strange town blamed him for something they didn't even understand.

No wonder Santa had a policy of staying out of Greater World affairs.

Julka hurried out of the Burger King. More cars were coming in, all of them with families inside, and everyone looking miserable.

She understood how snow could make people miserable— she got tired of it herself, long about May—but she never understood how anyone minded the first snowfall of the year, particularly one as dramatic as this one had been. Yes, it was cold; yes, the wind was harsh; but oh, it was always so beautiful.

That's what these people—all of them—seemed to be missing: The very beauty of living.

She cut across the parking lot, then went to the side of the health club. She only gave a cursory glance around her to make certain no one was watching—these people were so sour that they probably wouldn't accept real magic if they saw it.

Then she crouched, and sprang upward, using all those

magical muscles she had gotten when she got this assignment. She floated up to the roof. The sleigh shimmered ever so slightly, its outline only visible up close, and then only as a cutout against the sky.

She stepped inside, and winced at the stench of peppermint. Delbert was standing at the counter in the back, making a chocolate peppermint banana smoothie. She didn't even have to check her watch. The appearance of the smoothie meant it was now officially afternoon.

"Took you long enough," he said.

She ignored that. He said it every single time she came back in the sleigh. Sometimes the statement was accurate, and sometimes it wasn't. This time, it probably was.

She went over the array of cobbled together computer and magical equipment near the guidance system, and took her seat.

"We need to find someone," she said.

Delbert swallowed the smoothie in one long gulp, then wiped the brownish stain off his face. "Not our job," he said— or rather, mumbled. His mouth was still full of smoothie.

She hated the equipment. It looked like three 1950s television sets combined with a steam engine, rope, and a calliope. It had been designed by Santa hundreds of years ago, and modified every century or so. It hadn't gotten this century's modification because the fairies who designed the system were at war, and Santa didn't want to get involved.

The fairies were, so far as she knew, one of the few groups that could easily combine technology and magic. Santa had relied on them for his entire career. Until now.

She put her hands on the screen. She didn't have the magic to do a Santa-time search, where all she had to do was think of the person and end up with the name, address, personal history and current Naughty/Nice ranking. Instead, she had to use the screen as a window into the camera mounted on the sleigh's runners.

"I want this thing airborne," she said.

"Good," Delbert said. "We going back to work?"

"We're ahead of schedule," she reminded him.

"We still have 35 houses to go," he said.

"And five days allotted. We can do 35 houses in a morning."

"What happened out there?" he asked.

"Just get this thing in the air," she said.

He didn't argue. She was nominally in charge, even if he was an S-Elf. He was an S-Elf on double-secret forever probation, and he would probably never be in charge of anything ever again.

So he moved across the small cockpit to his little chair. Santa's sleigh had gorgeous benches and seats that molded to your frame. The back-up sleighs were utilitarian because they needed room for food storage, sleeping compartments (uncomfortable and dangerous sleeping compartments, which was why the advance team had a hotel budget), clothing, and other supplies.

Delbert's hands moved over what looked, to Julka, like a smooth countertop, and the sleigh shuddered. There were only two reasons an S-Elf had to be on a sleigh. The first was to test —as realistically as possible—Santa's entry into the various houses, and the second was to fly the sleighs. Only S-Elves had the encoding (some of the more scientific types said DNA, but others believed it was just a magical quirk) to get the sleighs in the air.

The sleigh wobbled and tumbled, and then righted itself. Delbert had had too much peppermint and was flying impaired. But Julka wasn't going to report him—at least not yet. Because if she did, then they might send a replacement, and she wouldn't be able to get away with...what? She wasn't sure what she was trying to get away with.

She just knew it was something.

She peered in the glass screen, which bubbled outward just a bit, distorting the images of rooftops, roads, and snow, snow, snow. Crews worked everywhere, repairing power lines or putting up signs telling people to stay away from lines.

No wonder people looked so sad. She hadn't quite realized the extent of the devastation before. The North Pole knew how to deal with snow from September to May; apparently here, in New England, they did not.

Then she saw what she was looking for: a flatbed truck with snow equipment. It was parked on a road in front of a house, and there he was, in the driveway with a snow blower, sending fresh wet snow in an arc onto what had probably been the lawn.

"There," she said, pointing.

"Can't," Delbert said. "No kids. Not this year, and probably not next."

"I don't care about the roof," she said. "I want to talk to the guy with the snow blower."

"You know that's not allowed," Delbert said.

"And you know if you were right, we couldn't get hotel rooms with the Greater World money that we're earning. I want to land on his lawn."

"He doesn't have a lawn," Delbert said. "That's a pile of

snow. And if we land anywhere near the removal equipment, snow will land on us and make us visible."

"So land on the other side," she said, not hiding her exasperation.

"Why is this so important to you?" he asked.

"It just is," she said. And she realized that was her answer. She couldn't leave their parting like it had been. She needed to talk with the handsome man one more time.

Delbert sighed and ran his hand on that countertop. The sleigh veered slightly to the left, making Julka lose her vision of the street and the snow blower. Then the sleigh settled out and hovered its way down, using its mechanical rudders.

The sleigh landed near that nifty staircase. Julka got out of the sleigh on the far side and sank into the snow up to her knees. She cursed (hoped Delbert didn't hear her since cursing outside the sleigh was a reportable offense), and used her rooftop magic to skim along the top of the snow to a side street. Then she brushed herself off as best she could, and walked down the icy street as if she had come from the Burger King.

She wasn't quite sure how to play this. "Yoo-hoo!" seemed to casual. "Hi!" probably impossible to hear over that blower. Walking up behind the handsome man and tapping him on the shoulder would probably scare him to death.

So she waited at the edge of the cleared-off area, and waited until he shut down the blower midway through the job, probably to take a short rest.

"Um," she said, wishing she had planned this better. "Excuse me?"

He still jumped like she had screamed at him. He turned

around fast, nearly lost his balance on the ice, and had to use the handles of the snow blower to catch himself.

"Um," he said. "Hi."

He sounded confused. Indeed, he was looking at her as if he wasn't sure if she was real.

She smiled at him and walked (carefully) up the slick driveway. "I just…you're a banker right?"

He let out a small sigh, and then shook his head. "No, I'm not a banker. I'm not anything really. I'm retired."

Judging from his tone of voice, she had asked the wrong thing. But she had committed herself to this, and she wasn't going to back off.

"Retired?" she asked. "I thought only really old people retired."

He smiled. The smile was small, reluctant, as if he didn't smile all that often. "It's a nice way of saying I quit."

So she had said something wrong again. Maybe reading and studying customs wasn't quite the same as understanding them.

"Oh," she said. "I thought in New England that retiring was mandatory at a certain age."

He frowned, then barked out a laugh. "In New England?"

"That's where we are, right?"

"Yes, but—where are you from?"

She couldn't answer that. She had to give the company's stock answer, which she felt wasn't complete enough. "Up north," she said.

"Canada?" he asked. "I thought Canadians knew about the United States. After all, we're kinda hard to miss."

"Yes," she said, "I mean, no. I mean, you are hard to miss."

She couldn't keep going in this direction. She was really

screwing up. She understood the difference between the United States and New England, she thought, but apparently not well enough.

"I just came to talk to you after lunch—those people were so strange. They said you did something wrong, but they didn't know what."

"They just need someone to blame," he said. Then he rubbed a gloved hand over his face. "That came out wrong. It came out like I'm accusing them. I'm not. It's just—"

"You retired," she said, still not entirely understanding what that meant.

"Yes," he said.

"And you've been spending the last few—months? Years? Being nice to them."

"No," he said sadly. "I've just been trying to fit in, and that won't work."

Then he shrugged, and said, "But you didn't come here to talk about that, did you?"

"I..." her voice trailed off. She didn't have a plausible lie. She had never been good at lying, even when she was supposed to for Santa or the kids.

So she pulled off her mitten and stuck out her hand. "I'm Julka."

"Marshall." He took her hand, but didn't shake it.

"Hi," she said, and blushed.

"Hi," he said, and shifted just a little. He hadn't let go of her hand yet.

She liked the way his hand felt, bigger and warmer than hers, enveloping hers altogether. Her eyes met his, and something shivered through her. Something better than nice.

He seemed to feel it too, because his eyes brightened. "I'd ask you to dinner," he said, "but after that lunch—"

"I know," she said. "I made a pig of myself."

"No, really," he said. "It's not that. How about coffee? It's really cold and we could have some coffee. Although I think most places aren't open. Half the town has lost power."

"Do you have power?" she asked. Besides power over her. Because he still held her hand and she didn't mind. She always minded when a man held her hand too long. And some of the elves were just plain gropey, which she didn't like at all.

"Um." Marshall glanced over his shoulder at the house. It looked way high up from here, with its odd mixture of Tudor and Colonial—and its seemingly perfect roof. "I do have power. I can make us coffee."

Her eyebrows went up. "This is your house?"

He nodded. "I thought you knew that."

She shook her head. No kids, Delbert had said. Not this year, and probably not next.

"So you're not married?" she blurted.

"No," Marshall said. That grip on her hand remained loose. The question didn't seem to bother him. "No girlfriends either. Not for the last year or so."

She wanted to say How lonely, but then she hadn't had a special fella for years now and she wasn't lonely. (Was she?) She had grown up with most of the guys at the North Pole, and they held no mystery for her.

She wanted mystery. She wanted difference. That was why she wanted to travel.

"I should say I'm sorry to hear that," she said, "but I'm not."

Then she smiled. She usually wasn't that forward. In fact, she couldn't ever remember being that forward, especially with a guy she knew nothing about.

"I can make you coffee inside," he said, "Or bring it out if you think that's too bold."

"It's not too bold," she said.

"It'll take maybe ten minutes to finish the driveway. If you don't mind."

"I don't mind," she said.

He smiled at her, then slowly let go of her hand. She felt the loss, not just of his warmth, but of him. She stepped back out of the way. She wished she had the skills some of the elves did. Snow removal with the snap of a finger. But her own magic was odd: seeing solutions when other people didn't even know there were problems. And the added magic she had gotten for the rooftops job hadn't helped at all.

He turned his back on her and started up the snow blower. As he went forward, someone grabbed her arm. She eeped. She didn't see anything. But she smelled peppermint and stale elf sweat.

Delbert.

"Hey," he said. "What is all this? You're not supposed to fraternize."

She could barely hear him over the snow blower, and she couldn't see him at all. He had on his invisibility shield, the same kind of shield that Santa used when a kid stumbled on him in the middle of the night. Only S-Elves could use an invisibility shield, but she'd sure like to try, if nothing else than to get rid of Delbert.

"Leave me alone," she said in the direction of the hand gripping her arm. She could see a Delbert-sized opening snow drift created by the blower. He had apparently barreled through. He had probably even left tracks all the way back to the invisible sleigh. Delbert really was not the brightest elf in the workshop.

"No," he said, tugging on her arm. "We're going to get in trouble."

And he couldn't afford any more trouble.

"If something goes wrong, I'll tell the truth," she said. "This is all my idea."

Behind her, the blower sounded louder. It was moving in a different direction. For some reason, that made her nervous. She started to turn—

When an arc of cold snow coated her. Her and Delbert.

———

Marshall was moving too fast. He hadn't been thinking. (Well, he had been thinking. Of Julka, not of anything else. Julka and coffee and the fact that she had found him, all on her own, and that she seemed nervous and she let him hold her hand and jeez, he felt like he was thirteen, only he hadn't felt this way when he was thirteen because he hadn't been able to get up enough nerve to talk to a girl, let alone touch her, or do anything until he was much, much older. College, really, and then only because he had met girls who were also interested in math and didn't mind awkwardness—and there he was, not thinking again.)

Anyway, he hadn't been thinking about blowing snow or the powerful machine vibrating under his hands. He had been hurrying so he could get to that coffee, and hurrying never really did anyone any good. He kept going in this kinda fugue state until he heard the blower go crunch, and then make a growly noise that wasn't normal.

That caught his attention. He had probably hit some kind of decorative rock—which he really had to remove come spring. He backed the blower up, turned it sideways to get it out of the awkward position it was in, and then turned again —and walloped poor Julka with a mound of snow.

His face flushed so hot he could have powered the entire block. He shut off the blower so he could apologize (even though she did look cute, standing there in her red not-elf costume, with snow frosting her hair, eyelashes, and cheekbones) and that was when he realized that there was something else beside her.

Somehow the snow had formed a weird kinda snow man next to her. Only it looked vaguely like an unfinished Santa. Marshall had never seen the snow do anything like that, and he figured it was probably like the ways that clouds formed animal shapes—at least, he thought that until the Santa shape moved and cursed in definitively not Santa-like language.

"Hey!" the Santa shape said in a burly male voice. "We're standing here."

Its (his?) violent movement made half of the snow fall (off? Was there something to fall off of?), leaving a partial Santa shape that reminded Marshall of nothing more than a half-eaten unfrosted Santa sugar cookie.

"Shh, Delbert," Julka said, not moving her lips. But she wasn't as quiet as she clearly thought she was, because Marshall heard her.

"There really is someone there?" he asked.

"No!" she and the male voice said in unison. Then Julka turned her head and glared at the half-Santa shape.

Marshall looked at him (it?) too, and realized that just past it was a roundish opening in the snow drift, and footprints in the snow that came from the yard somewhere.

This time, Marshall couldn't blame it on tiredness or on not having food or on his imagination. This time, he knew he was seeing something odd, and he knew it for two reasons:

One, other people in the Burger King had seen Julka. (And besides, he'd been struggling with ketchup-flavored burps ever since he left, so he had clearly been to Burger King.)

And two, if they had seen Julka, and she had come here (and she had, he knew it, because he could still conjure the sensation of her hand in his), then she was talking to the half-Santa shape, and that meant she saw it too.

In fact, that meant that she knew what it was.

"Someone want to tell me what's going on here?" Marshall asked.

"No," the male voice said.

"Delbert!" Julka clearly reprimanded the voice, but Marshall couldn't tell what for. For talking? For standing there? For being rude?

"Just...just...just fix it," she was saying as if that thought broke her heart.

"I can't," the voice (Delbert?) said. "I had most of my S-Elf privileges removed."

Julka rolled her eyes. "Okay, then," she said, grabbing the air in front of her and pulling.

As she did, the air waved, like a tablecloth in the breeze. Marshall wasn't sure what caused that effect. He wasn't sure he wanted to know. But his mind didn't linger on it long, because as she tugged, a round man appeared.

He had a white beard and white hair, and he was wearing

sweats that clearly needed washing, and a too-small T-shirt that said, Lobstermen do it with nets. He looked like Santa but not really.

"You're not supposed to see me," this Delbert guy said to Marshall.

"Well, I think the reindeer missed that sleigh," Julka said, rolling her eyes.

She clearly wasn't making the comment to Marshall, who was still having a bit of trouble comprehending all of this.

"It's not my fault, really," Delbert said. "I'm supposed to have the power to make you not remember seeing me, but they took my privileges away from me, and now I can't do that. I mean, how can you blame me?"

"I can blame you," Julka said softly.

Marshall wanted to ask who "they" were, and what the "privileges" were, but he wasn't sure he would like the answer. The last time he heard the words "they" and "privileges" in an incoherent context, "they" referred to the mental health hospital staff and "privileges" meant walking the hospital grounds.

Which he didn't want to think about. Because if Delbert was off the hospital grounds, did that mean Julka was too? And how come Delbert had looked invisible? No one could become invisible. Marshall firmly believed that. If he didn't, he would need to be led along a sidewalk on the grounds, heading toward the hospital proper.

"So," Delbert was saying to Marshall, "can you just like pretend that you didn't see me? Because if an unauthorized someone ever sees me again, then I'm going to be sent home and never be allowed out again."

There it was. Hospital grounds, couched in the vague

terms. Marshall closed his eyes and sighed. No wonder people emphasized the power of "nice" where Julka lived. "Nice" meant that folks with mental health issues had to learn how to get along.

It explained why she had looked so happy when she had come into Burger King. Freedom did that for folks.

It also explained why she was here. She had nowhere else to go, except back.

And somehow, he was going to have to be the one to get her there. How on Earth was he supposed to find out where she had come from without tipping his hand? The only clue she had given him was that she was from up north, but he wasn't even sure he could trust that. Did folks with mental health issues have a good sense of direction?

He had no idea.

He held up his hands as if he was being robbed. Maybe he was. Robbed of his delusions.

"I'll make sure no one knows I saw you," Marshall said to Delbert. "I promise."

"You don't have to promise him anything," Julka said. "He screwed up. He shouldn't have gotten out of the sleigh."

Then she clapped both hands over her mouth as Delbert slapped her arm.

"I didn't say that," he said. "I didn't. If they blame me for that, I'm going to give you up. I mean it, along with all that weird behavior. And fraternizing. You shouldn't fraternize. I told you nothing good would come of it."

Fraternize. Apparently he meant with Marshall. Apparently, these two weren't even allowed to talk to people.

Marshall let out a small sigh. A perfect capper to a perfectly bad week. He leaned back, shut off the snow blower, and tucked the key in his pocket. Then he almost put his hands up again. That robbing metaphor stuck with him, probably because he felt like he'd been robbed.

"Look, you guys are clearly far from home, and in a strange place and I'm sure that's not comfortable...."

Lord, he was babbling. Julka was staring at Marshall with such disappointment that he felt worse than he had a moment ago. He stopped talking altogether.

He had encountered yet another situation that he didn't know how to handle. He had no idea how many more of them he could take.

———

J ulka's breath caught. Marshall thought she was crazy. She had been warned about this reaction in all of her Greater World classes. If she talked too much about the North Pole or exhibited too much magical behavior, the people of the Greater World would dismiss her as a crazy person.

But she didn't want Marshall to think her crazy. She had liked the way he looked at her before, the interest in his eyes, the way that he smiled at her, the touch of his hand on hers. She had liked that a lot. More than a lot, actually. She had been looking forward to coffee and conversation, and stretching those 35 houses into five days worth of work, and getting to know Marshall and maybe putting in a request to meet the folks who ran the New England advance team—the entire team, not just the Entry Access Quality Control section. Maybe she could be assigned here permanently. She liked the snow, after all.

She hadn't realized all of those dreams had been in her

mind just since lunch until Marshall looked at her like she wasn't right in the head. If she could righteously punch Delbert right now, she would. But he had just been trying to save her from herself.

And failing.

But he was correct: it was her fault. She had wanted a bunch of things that were forbidden to her. And she was going to get into trouble for it.

Then she frowned.

She was going to get into trouble for it. Anyway. That's the word she was missing. She was going to get in trouble anyway, so why not go for broke?

It was better than finding an S-Elf who would make Marshall forget he even met her. She had momentarily been willing to follow that rule, and the pain in her chest—in her heart—had been severe.

She liked this man. She more than liked this man. This man felt—she didn't even have the word. More appropriate? Better? Right? He felt right for her.

So she was going to go for broke. And if they decided to punish her at the North Pole, so be it. Nothing could feel worse than that moment when she had asked Delbert to make Marshall forget him. Her. Them.

Make Marshall forget them.

She shoved the invisibility shield at Delbert, and hit him with it in the stomach. She liked to think that was an accident, but it probably wasn't.

He caught it and his hands immediately disappeared. Hers didn't when she held the dang thing, but Delbert's did. Of course, someone who didn't even believe in magic probably wouldn't notice the difference.

She extended her hand to Marshall. "Come with me."

He looked at her cautiously, that what's-she-going-to-do-now look in his eye, the one that people got when she misbehaved. He hadn't used that on her before.

She had to change the look by no longer earning it.

"Please," she said.

He glanced at Delbert, blinked, and frowned. Marshall had clearly seen the missing hands. In fact, Delbert was holding the shield in front of his legs, so from the waist down, a circle of him had disappeared, leaving only the outside of his thighs, his ankles and his shoes visible.

No one could miss that. She wasn't sure how anyone could justify it to themselves, but no one could miss it.

She extended her hand just a little farther. Marshall eyed it like it might bite him, when before he had clearly enjoyed touching her.

She held her breath.

He stepped forward and took her hand firmly in his own. "All right," he said. "Where do you want to go?"

He didn't know what he expected—maybe that she would lead him to his truck or to the vehicle she had stolen (because if she had escaped from an institution, she couldn't have one of her own, right?). The one thing he did know was this: He hadn't expected her to lead him through the hole in the snow.

She dragged him around Delbert, and she walked into the hole. Marshall followed.

The first thing that he noticed was that the hole was a

Delbert-sized hole, and that the footprints—heading toward his driveway—were Delbert-sized footprints. But they were the only pair of prints. Marshall saw no sign of Julka's dainty prints, the ones she was now leaving on the way to— what? He couldn't tell. But he did see some flat deep marks in the snow, marks that looked like they were made by giant skis.

He felt a shiver run down his back that had nothing to do with the cold. Was someone playing a prank on him? Was this a trick to get the terrible investment banker out of the neighborhood? And if so, why do it now? Why not wait until Christmas?

He was feeling paranoid. Heck, no. He was paranoid. But he had to admit, if only to himself, that this afternoon—ever since he had seen Julka in Burger King (if not before) was extremely strange.

Still, it would be impossible to do such a thing in this storm, on the eve of Halloween.

He didn't say anything. He let her pull him to the marks in the snow. Of course, he did. And he felt really sad. Because he had liked her more than he had liked any woman he ever met, more than he had liked anyone he had ever met. He had found her intriguing and beautiful in her non-elfish way, and just odd enough to make her interesting to him.

And he had sacrificed that for her, so she could have a good trip here, thinking the memory would be enough for him. Then she had shown up here at his house, and he actually had hope for something more, something that would be—he didn't know, more than coffee, surely, more than a simple afternoon talking.

He only knew that he could have gazed in her eyes forever.

He reached her side only a second later. He wondered where the joke would go now.

Then she reached up and mimed opening a door.

———

The smell of peppermint and spoiled veal wafted out of the sleigh, so strong that it made Julka choke. She hadn't realized just how filthy the interior of the sleigh had gotten.

But, she was going to get in trouble anyway, so she was in all the way. She was taking this risk.

Even if no one else wanted her to.

Marshall no longer looked at her like she was crazy. Now he looked at her with that sadness he'd had at the Burger King. The sadness he'd had when they talked about his life. And that made her feel even worse.

"Come with me," she said one more time, and climbed the flight of invisible steps into the sleigh.

———

He still held her hand. His hand rose up as she climbed a set of steps he couldn't see.

He wasn't sure why he couldn't see them; he just knew that he couldn't. Usually he could see clear plastic or whatever it was that made the steps impossible to see against that backdrop of new fallen snow. But his eyes were really off this afternoon.

He couldn't see a thing.

Half of Julka seemed to disappear into the air. But he was

holding her hand, so he knew this wasn't some optical illusion.

He felt around with the toe of his boot until he found the invisible stair, then he put the bottom of his boot on it and slid his foot forward. The toe hit the next stair, but it still looked to him like he was standing on nothing.

The illusion made him oddly uncomfortable.

The smell of peppermint mixed with rotting garbage made his stomach turn. When he reached the top of the third step, he could see Julka, standing inside a—what? He didn't have the word for it. The interior of a small RV? If it was an RV, it was a 1950s Christmas-themed RV crossed with a 1950s version of a spacecraft or an airplane cockpit.

He felt dizzy, and he realized he was holding his breath.

It was that stench.

Then he leaned back out of the door, and peered at the exterior.

There was no exterior. Only a blank spot where there should've been a view of the hedgerow between his property and the neighbor's, and the curve in the road, and from this vantage, the tip of another neighbor's house.

"Come on," she said for the third time.

Third time's the charm, his mom always used to say. He wondered what she would think now. His mom hadn't had a lot of imagination. She didn't even understand imaginary numbers, which made his mathematics brain hurt. A mathematician needed imagination, and his mom (face it, his parents) had none.

Although they had been proud of him. Investment banker, venture capitalist. They hadn't lived to see the collapse, didn't know about his loss of reputation, had no idea how lonely he would become.

They had always imagined him with a family—his father had said as much before the cancer took him—and that was their only disappointment. They had passed on before seeing grandchildren.

Or seeing their son lapse into complete insanity.

He stepped inside.

And immediately hit his head on the top of the door. The pain sent a shiver through him. He grabbed his forehead with his free hand. The door's opening had to be really low for him to hit his head because he was not quite six feet tall. And everything in America was built to accommodate a six-foot tall man.

But Julka had an accent, and she had made it clear she wasn't from here.

She was from up north. And she had looked a bit confused when he mentioned Canada, so maybe it wasn't that up north, but a different up north.

And she was wearing a red Santa/elf costume.

His stomach twisted—and not from the smell. Oddly enough, he was getting used to that. His stomach twisted because he was getting suspicious.

He didn't like what he was thinking.

He hadn't thought about impossible things since he got his doctorate, when he realized that impossible imaginings and mathematical theories weren't practical enough to help him survive in the real world. He'd moved to statistical analysis and mathematical systems and economics, and had made a fortune, but had screwed up his life.

So, for a moment anyway, he was going to settle on one

impossible thing: A pretty non-elf woman in a Christmas costume on the day before Halloween, standing inside an invisible RV decorated like Santa's 1950 Christmas nightmare.

Marshall stood up slowly so that he didn't hit his head on the rounded ceiling. It looked like the ceiling in a camper, not the ceiling in an RV. Modern RVs, they looked like small houses. There was nothing house-like about this place. It was crammed with stuff, including some filthy t-shirts that had crude sayings on them, often with drawings. They, like everything else he'd seen so far, were Delbert-sized.

In one corner, there was a shelf covered with dainty things. That had to belong to Julka.

Marshall moved in a slow circle, taking it all in. Could this be an hallucination? Those usually didn't come with touch and stink. An illusion? Again, those were usually aimed at the eye, not the other sense. And he was wrong about the stink. It didn't just use up one sense. It imposed on two. He could taste that rot. Peppermint would never be a happy fragrance for him again.

Julka just watched him, looking a little tense.

"Okay," he said after a moment. "My first response is that you gotta explain this."

She opened her mouth, but he held up his hand so that she couldn't speak.

"My second response is that you don't dare explain this." His heart was pounding. "Because if you explain it, then I'm going to have to think about it, and if I think about it, then I'm going to have accept some things that I'm not willing to accept —or, at least, something that I haven't accepted for oh, twenty-some years."

Her mouth closed, and she tilted her head, looking both bemused and worried.

"Not," he said, "that I'm close-minded or anything. It's just that I'm—oh, God—not willing to change cherished beliefs, which makes me close-minded, I guess, or maybe just adult, because if I take this at face value, then that means Santa is real, and if Santa is real, then all of those science courses I took, all of those courses that I believed in, they would be wrong."

Julka raised a finger, as if she were going to say something. And he really should let her talk, but he couldn't stop babbling, because if he stopped, then she would tell him what he was seeing, and that would be a bad thing.

A very bad thing.

"And if the science courses are wrong, well, that's less serious than the math courses being wrong, because I believe in math, and it is a mathematical impossibility for one man to circle the globe in 24 hours and drop off the right toys at the right house without anyone seeing him. Just on the time factor alone. There aren't enough minutes in the day. There just aren't. And that's for the flying and the landing. That's not really counting the time it would take to squeeze down a chimney."

Then his breath caught. He first saw her on rooftops. Looking at chimneys. He'd seen her kick a chimney.

But he couldn't think about that right now. So he kept talking. Because if he let her talk, then she might say something sensible. (How could there be anything sensible about this?) And he would have to listen, and if he listened, then—

"Maybe I can deal with the loss of science," he said, "but the loss of math—well, that's like the final straw. Because I devoted my life to math. Until this moment, I understood

116

math. I have always understood math. That's why I retired when I couldn't convince the guys in my office that the way they were floating on one of those proverbial mathematical bubbles and those things didn't last, but if this is all true, well then, this bubble has lasted, and everything, everything, I know is wrong, and I really really really can't face that. Not right now."

Julka's shoulders drooped. He had disappointed her. Worse, he had hurt her somehow. He wasn't sure how, but he had.

"It's not about math," she started.

"Of course it's about math." He sounded even more panicked than he felt. He sounded terrified and wobbly and slightly off-the-beam. Maybe more than slightly off-the-beam. "Don't you understand? That's how I knew Santa wasn't real. I did the damn math."

"I understand math," Julka said, moving her hands just a little in a "calm down" gesture. Now she was treating him as if he was the one who was crazy, and maybe he was. This entire idea had left him so unsettled that off-the-beam was really the wrong way to describe it. Off his nut might've been better.

"Really," she said, taking a step toward him. "I love math. It was one of my best subjects in school, and I use it all the time, because I love organizing."

He almost said with a mathematician's sneer, That's not math. That's arithmetic. But he needed to shut up now. He needed to stop talking and let her say something.

"Math is a phenomenal thing," Julka was saying. "You can represent it with sticks on the simplest level—you know, one-plus-one-equals-two kinda thing. Then math starts getting really complex, and you have to imagine it and sometimes you

117

have to trust it, and there are pockets of it and corners of it that no one understands at all."

His breath caught. She did know math. Not arithmetic. Math.

"I have a hunch, if you come back home with me, you'll find some people who can explain the math and the science to you. It's elegant." She glanced at what looked like several old-fashioned TV sets, but through one of them, he could see the neighborhood. He could see his driveway.

Delbert was missing. Was that important?

"You're telling me that it's not magic. It's science." Marshall couldn't quite keep the sarcasm from his voice.

"I seem to recall reading a book when I was a kid that said that all science looks like magic to those who don't understand it," Julka said.

She was quoting Arthur C. Clarke. A science-fiction writer. One of Marshall's favorite writers when he was a kid. How long had it been since he had read something for fun?

How long had it been since he had fun?

Then he wondered if he was supposed to be wondering that. Was there something in this sleigh/RV/invisible thing that made him think thoughts he didn't want? That magicked him?

He sank into a nearby chair. It was large and it smelled of peppermint. He popped out of it quickly.

"So you're saying it's all science," Marshall repeated.

"I'm saying I don't know." Julka came closer to him. "But what if it is magic and not science? What's wrong with that?"

"It's not possible—"

"Most things aren't possible," she said. "Bumblebees aren't

possible, yet they exist. Soul mates aren't possible, yet people always say they found theirs."

She bit her bottom lip as if she had said something she hadn't planned on saying.

Soul mates. His parents said they were each other's soul mates and believed it too. He had done the math on that as well, and figured with billions of people on Earth that the odds of finding the one person who suited you were—well, billions to one. So he figured (but he never said to his parents) that everyone had a bunch of soul mates, and it was all chemical, and none of that explained the look in Julka's eyes.

The anticipation, with a bit of fear. The fact that her pupils were slightly dilated which, he had learned in some long-ago biology class, was a sign of attraction.

And it didn't explain how it bothered him to hurt her or to upset her or how he just wanted to take her hands in his and pull her forward and kiss her silly.

He'd never done anything that bold in his entire life.

"Why did you bring me here?" he asked softly.

She shrugged and looked away. "I was going to get in trouble anyway."

"For what?"

She bowed her head. "Fraternizing."

"With me?"

"With anyone who wasn't, you know, someone I had to talk to, like one of the employees at Burger King."

Marshall frowned. "You'd get in trouble for talking to me. Why?"

"We have illusions to keep up," she said, head still down, voice almost a whisper. "The entire world thinks Santa does this alone."

No, Marshall wanted to say, we're taught that he has elves. And then Marshall realized that they were taught about the elves in the workshop, not elves outside of the workshop. Not elves on the rooftops of Connecticut.

"You were scouting out chimneys," he said, less as a question and more as a realization.

"No, not exactly," she said. "I'm tasked with looking for the best entry locations on the proper houses."

Corporate speak. She was actually using corporate speak.

"How big is this organization?" Marshall asked.

She shrugged. "I don't know. Are you asking money or personnel?"

"Both, I guess," he said, suddenly unable to visualize paying for everything he knew about the fictional Santa.

"I'm not privy to the money side," she said, "but it's huge. And we have millions of employees worldwide, not all of them human."

Not all of them human. He tried not to let his brain turn to mush at that statement. "You mean reindeer, and stuff."

"Elves," she said. "They're not human. Delbert's not human."

"He's an elf?" Marshall asked.

"He's an S-Elf," Julka said. "From Santa's line. Those are the most important elves of all."

"Wow," Marshall said, believing it, then wondering if he should believe it, and then wondering if the sleigh (this was a sleigh, right?) made him believe it, and then wondering if he should believe that the sleigh made him believe.

So he gave up wondering at all.

"But you're human," he said, and it was more of a hope than a question.

She nodded. "A lot of families got hired real early on to humanize the whole procedure and most of them stayed. My family goes back twenty-five generations at the North Pole."

He did the arithmetic in his head: Twenty-five generations, at roughly twenty years per generation, was—

"Five hundred years?" he blurted.

"Give or take," she said.

"So you grew up at the North Pole?" he asked. "I thought it's desolate there."

"It's not the North Pole that you can travel to," she said. "It's like this sleigh. We have a different North Pole that you can access—or rather, I can access—through your North Pole."

His North Pole. He'd never seen the North Pole. Either one, actually.

"And you now work as what—Santa's advance team?" he asked.

"Kinda," she said. "I'm probably going to get fired for this."

"For bringing me here," he said.

She nodded miserably.

"What happens when you get fired?" he asked.

She shrugged a shoulder. "I'll probably have to go back to training school, and they'll find me a job at the Pole. I really, really, really wanted to spend my time in the Greater World."

"Which is—?"

"Your world," she said. "I wanted to man one of the advance headquarters, you know, have a permanent place here."

"And you risked all that to talk to me?" he asked. "Why?"

"I don't know." She raised her head. "You just seemed important somehow."

"Important to...?"

"Me," she said miserably. "Important to me."

No one had thought him important for years. Not since his parents died. And then, he wasn't their main priority. They were each other's main priority. He was second on their list and had been from the beginning. He had known that almost as soon as he started breathing.

"Why would I be important to you?" he asked. "We just met."

"I know," she said. "It's stupid, isn't it?"

He took her hands. She was trembling.

"No," he said. "No. It's not stupid."

He wanted to say it was an honor, but that actually sounded like he was dismissing it. And if he said You're important to me too, it would sound like he was just trying to make her feel better, and he wasn't.

"I'm standing here," he said, "and you're making me rethink everything I've ever known, and honestly, I'm not fleeing, which is what I usually do when I'm challenged. I turn away. And I don't want to."

Her gaze met his. Her eyes were big and blue and incredibly beautiful. "Why?"

"Because," he whispered, "I found another place where the math doesn't work."

"What—?" she asked.

"Soul mates," he said. "It's mathematically ridiculous."

She nodded, and tried to pull her hands from his.

"But I've never felt anything like this before," he said. "So right, so perfect, as if we were made for each other."

Her eyes filled with tears, but they didn't fall. He leaned forward and kissed the corner of one eye, tasting salt, tasting her. Then he showered kisses down the side of her face until she tilted her head toward him.

Their mouths met, and tentatively, hesitantly, they kissed. Then the kiss got deeper, and he finally understood what his parents talked about: that rightness, that sense he had found his other half, that sense of perfection, of—

"Oh, no," said a male voice. Delbert's voice. "Now I really will have to report this."

The sleigh rocked as Delbert climbed inside. He put both hands on the side of the door as if he was blocking someone's escape, but Julka didn't know whose.

It certainly wouldn't be her. She didn't want to move. She hadn't wanted to break the kiss, but Marshall had done so, looking startled—again.

She almost brought her fingers to her mouth in amazement. She had never been kissed like that. She had never felt anything like that before. Never.

And she wanted to feel it again.

"Report?" Marshall asked, sounding a bit unsettled. "To whom?"

"You'd think it'd be to the big guy," Delbert said, "but he doesn't handle small personnel matters. Still, this is one of those things. I don't like reporting anyone for fraternization, Julka, especially since I know how it can go, but I'm on double-secret forever probation, and if I don't and they find out, I'll never be able to leave the North Pole again. I'm sorry."

He sounded sorry. She had never seen him look so upset,

actually. He reached over to that flat countertop area and touched a red button she'd never noticed before.

And then he vanished.

"What?" Marshall said. "What was that? Is he still here?"

"No," Julka said. She felt heavy suddenly. Her legs wouldn't support her, and she had to grope for one of the chairs before she sat down. She had known it was a risk bringing Marshall here, but somehow she hadn't thought Delbert would report her. Maybe he wouldn't have without the kiss. Or maybe he was just giving her a chance to come to her senses.

Which she hadn't.

She still didn't regret this, no matter what the consequences.

"Where did he go?" Marshall asked.

"Headquarters," she said miserably. "They're going to bring the goon squad here, and they'll clean up after me."

"How will they do that?" Marshall asked.

She didn't want to tell him, although it really didn't matter if she told him. None of this would matter to him in…oh, five minutes or so.

But she didn't want to lie to him, not even now, not when she could leap back into his arms and kiss him senseless until the goon squad got here.

"They'll wipe your memory," she said. "Delbert should have done it, but they've limited his powers."

She had asked Delbert to do it, but that was before the kiss. It had broken her heart then. It would destroy her now.

Oddly, it felt like she had known this man her entire life— or maybe, it felt like she would know this man her entire life. Better than anyone else.

But that was going away too.

Her hands were shaking.

"They'll make me forget?" Marshall asked. "They can do that? With magic?"

"I don't know how they do it," she said tiredly. "I just know that they do. S-Elves can. Santa can. To protect the myth, you know. It's all about protecting the myth."

"From what?" Marshall asked.

She shook her head. "We're supposed to control the message."

"And the message is that pretty women can't kiss men they're interested in?"

"No," she said. "We can't fraternize. You're not part of the community. You can't know about us, and I told."

She worse than told. She showed him everything that she could in the short time allowed. He'd been inside the sleigh. No one got inside the sleigh. No one except people with clearance.

She hadn't even had clearance until a few months ago.

"I can't forget this," he said. "This is life-changing."

"I know," she said. And she did. That was why the secrets never got out. They made sensible men kiss women like her. They made sensible men deny their belief in science for a grasp at the hope of Christmas magic. They made—

"No," Marshall said. "You don't know. You think I'm talking about Santa. I'm talking about you."

She froze, just for a moment. What had he said? Her? Really? He found her life-changing like she had found him life-changing?

"I can't forget you," he said. "You're the best thing that has ever happened to me, and I mean ever. Even if I never see you again, I can't forget you."

"They won't let that happen," she said, resisting the urge to look at her watch. She wanted to know how much time was left before the goon squad arrived, but she didn't want to know at the same time. "You can't remember me. Only insiders know this stuff. I should've thought it through."

"Insiders," he said, kneeling in front of her and taking her shoulders in his hands. His hands were warm, strong. She liked his hands. "You mean people who work at the North Pole—your North Pole."

"Yes," she said.

He kissed her. "Julka, you're brilliant."

He let go of her and bounded over to that countertop where the red button still glowed. He slapped his hand on the button and nothing happened. Then he kept pounding.

"I don't know how to make you hear me," he shouted at the screens, "but give me a job. Surely you have use for a mathematician who understands business and statistics and real money management. I can streamline your business. I can make it more efficient. I know how to save money without changing personnel or making you lose any of your goodwill. I can—"

His voice cut out first. And then he shimmered. And finally, he disappeared.

Julka ran to the countertop. The button was gone. Delbert was gone. Marshall was gone.

Something had happened, and she didn't entirely understand it.

Correction: she didn't understand it at all.

———————

One minute he was standing in that weird 1950s RV sleigh, the next he was inside a badly decorated 1950s office, complete with single-pane windows frosting up against the cold outside, a humidifier trying to keep moisture in the dry air, a blond desk and matching chair, and a square console television set in the corner, its bulging screen showing the inside of that 1950s RV sleigh, with Julka frantically pressing the countertop he had just been touching.

The room smelled of coffee and cookies. The walls were covered in flocked candy cane wallpaper, and someone had wrapped a green ribbon around the back of the couch. A poinsettia sat on the blond wood end table, and the happy faces of cartoon carolers decorated the window above the door.

The transition made Marshall feel dizzy, but he felt weirdly comfortable too, for the first time in years. It took only a moment for him to understand why: this was a corporate environment—a corporate environment decorated for Christmas (on the day before Halloween), but a corporate environment all the same.

He turned toward the desk. A woman of indeterminate age sat behind it. She had a beehive hairdo dyed so black that it looked like the color would smear on her fingers if she touched it. She wore a lot of make-up, also making it impossible to determine her age including bright red lipstick that matched her bright red fingernails. A cigarette that he couldn't smell smoldered in a red and green ashtray that said, "Keep the Happy in Christmas!"

The combination of the words "happy" and "Christmas"

collided in his head, and therefore, he wasn't surprised when the woman spoke to him in a working class English accent.

"So," she said, "you think you have something to offer Claus & Company."

Apparently, she wasn't at all surprised by his appearance. Apparently, she had something to do with it.

He bowed his head just a little. It had been a decade or more since he had had a job interview. There were no chairs on this side of the desk. He felt like he should have a hat in his hands—a supplicant.

"I've got more than a decade in finance," he said. "I know how to make companies more efficient—"

"We're familiar with you American efficiency types," she said. "You cut staff to the bone, get rid of markets that are underperforming, and while the business makes a profit, the customers are deeply dissatisfied. We are in the customer satisfaction business, not the profit business."

He nodded. He wasn't dressed for this. He didn't have his resume or any papers with him. All he had were his wits, which, he had to admit, were getting a bit tired on this day.

"I-I know," he said. "It's something I've decried for my entire career. I got let go from my finance job when I tried to convince the company that they were hurting the very people they were trying to help. I used statistics and math to show that a long-term view would make them more profitable down the road, and it would bring in more customers, and everyone would be happy, but that didn't—"

"Honestly, Mr. Collier, we at Claus & Company don't care about your Greater World concerns," the woman said. "What we care about is what you can bring to us."

Marshall opened his hands a little. "Normally, ma'am, I

research a company before I talk to anyone involved with it. But I've been a bit blindsided here. I didn't know you existed until today—"

"You knew," she said in a chiding tone. "Everyone knows about us. Then they 'grow up' and 'lose sight of childish things.' You were one of those, I suppose."

His cheeks flushed. "The real world—what you call the Greater World...?"

She nodded. That hair moved with her head like it weighed a ton.

"...it can be a harsh and disillusioning place." He shrugged. "I let it disillusion me."

"And still, you're here," she said, picking up that cigarette and tapping an inch of ash off the end. The cigarette got no shorter. "You can't be entirely disillusioned."

"Julka convinced me," he said, wondering if he should speak her name, wondering if he would get her in trouble. "Only a fool denies what's in front of him, and she placed it all in front of me."

"She's quite attractive, eh?" the woman asked.

They knew. They knew everything, and he was dancing around it all like a fool.

"I like her a lot," he said. "More than I've ever liked anyone. I won't lie to you, ma'am. The idea of losing the memory of this day, even if I never see her again, is more than I can bear."

"So you're just here to get the girl," the woman said.

He shook his head. "You people give others hope. Even if they don't want it, they brighten up for just one day. They smile for a moment. I've learned these last few years that those smiles are important."

The woman stared at him and tapped more ash off her cigarette.

"Yes," he said. "I'm here because of Julka, because she brought something bright and magical and wonderful into my life. I expect I won't see her again. I expect you to send me on my way. But please, don't make me forget her. Those moments —even if they're fleeting—are the most important thing in life."

The woman still stared at him. Didn't she have any emotions?

"I have been trying to make up for all I did at my previous work," he said. "I've been doing my best, but I'm flailing around. Being here would give me focus. It would make me remember that there are people behind the numbers. Even when the numbers are impossible."

The woman put the cigarette in her mouth and took a drag. He still couldn't smell the dang thing, which was a good thing; he didn't like the smell of cigarette smoke. But it was a bit freaky.

"If you came to work for us," she said, "you would get benefits. Your life would be extended by perhaps a century or more. You would be given small magic via spell that would have to be renewed annually. You would get housing and clothing and all of your needs provided for."

He swallowed. He'd been through these kinds of interviews before. He knew there was a "but" coming.

"But," she said rather loudly, "you won't be able to tell your family what you do, and when it becomes obvious that you're not aging at the same rate they are, you will have to forgo seeing them altogether. You won't be able to talk to your friends about this either. You will get two weeks annual vacation which you can take in the Greater World, but you cannot do so in the fall or over Christmas. The sacrifice is often greater than the average mortal can make."

He couldn't say anything about his friends. His friends had pretty much disowned him when he retired. The new friends that he could have had after that were mostly after his money. So he just said, "My family is gone."

"Well then." The woman stood, set down that weird cigarette, and extended her hand. "You're hired."

That surprised him too. What a surprising day. But the surprise wasn't enough to make him lose focus.

He shook the woman's hand.

"Thank you," he said, and he meant it. Who knew when he got up that morning that by the middle of the day he would be giving up everything, and realizing that by doing so, he was giving up nothing at all.

"You will go back to Julka and await your instructions," the woman said. "Congratulations. We at Claus & Company hope that our relationship with you is long and merry."

"Me, too," Marshall said. "Me too."

———————

Julka kept hitting the countertop.

"C'mon," she said. "I know someone can see me. What did you do with him? Take me to him. He has no idea what home is like. Please."

She had no idea where he was. Had Marshall hit the red button that was still pulsing there and had it sent him where Delbert was? Or did someone actually hear him make his offer, and take him to the North Pole somehow. She had no idea how that would work for a non-elf. Even elves had to use sleigh magic. Had Marshall somehow triggered something?

"Please," she said, not quite sure any more what she was begging for. "Please."

Her hand hurt from hitting the console. She was going to have to come up with something else. They had told her about an emergency way to contact the North Pole if something happened to Delbert, but she hadn't really paid attention. Nothing ever happened to elves. Particularly elves that stank of peppermint and elf sweat.

Then she realized she was smelling peppermint and elf sweat. She turned around. Delbert was watching her, his head tilted, looking amused.

"At first," he said, "I thought maybe you were one of those people who fell in crap and came out looking like gold. But the longer my conversation with HR went on, the more I realized you were sent to recruit someone. And damn, if you didn't manage it. You know, you could've told me."

She didn't know what he was referring to. Crap? Conversation? Recruit? "Told you what?"

"That you weren't here to inspect chimneys. I should've figured it out. You weren't the chimney inspecting type. And you got frustrated when there were too many pipes and not enough bricks. The usual chimney worker doesn't really care." He tugged on his shirt, pulling it down over his massive belly.

"I was too here to inspect chimneys," she said. "I didn't lie to you."

His eyebrows went up. "You mean that, don't you?"

"Yes, I mean that," she said.

He bit his lower lip, then rolled his eyes and sighed. "Ah. They sent you here on a test, and left it up to me to tell you."

"What?" she asked. She had been frustrated before he showed up. Now she was ready to grab him and shove his hand against the console (repeatedly) so she could find Marshall.

"That guy," Delbert said, "you know, the one you were kissing? Which I don't think they planned on, to tell the truth."

Her cheeks flushed, but she didn't care. "What about Marshall? Is he all right?"

"He's in Human Resources right now," Delbert said, "getting interviewed for his new job. They think you did great. He was a better catch than they expected, but they had to grill him. They didn't want him to show up just because he wanted to be in your pants."

"What?" she asked.

Delbert shrugged. "You were the one who wanted a real job, not some workshop management position. A chance to get out into the Greater World, you said. Well, the job choices are limited, but the best ones are the recruiters, because they can go anywhere. Only I'd never met one before, had you?"

It was taking Julka a few minutes to catch up. "You're saying they tested me. As a recruiter?"

"Yeah," Delbert said and grinned. "Although I'm really not sure they're going to want you to kiss each recruit to get him to come to the North Pole."

"I didn't kiss him because I was recruiting him," Julka said. "I like him. I have never kissed anyone like that before."

"Well," said a voice from beside her. "That's good to hear."

Marshall was standing there. He was wearing just a bit of

glitter—the kind that rubbed off flocked candy cane wallpaper. It got on everything.

She threw herself in his arms. "I'm sorry, I'm sorry, I'm sorry," she said. "I didn't know."

"I gathered that," Marshall said.

"They manipulated us into recruiting you. I didn't mean it," she said.

He pulled back just a little. "You don't want me to work at the North Pole?" he asked.

She didn't, not if it meant she was working here. But that wasn't what he meant, and she knew it. "I didn't know about the recruitment or the test."

"I know," he said.

"I really like you," she said.

"I know that too," he said.

"I...." want to spend the rest of my life with you. Never want to leave your side. All of that was too forward this soon, although it didn't feel soon.

"It's okay," he said, pulling her close again. "I like you too. I more than like you. It looks like I'm changing my entire life for you."

"No," she said. "You can't. You can't base a relationship on that."

"Is that what you want?" he asked. "A relationship?"

Her breath caught. "Don't you?"

He smiled. A real smile without sadness. "Of course I do," he said, and then he leaned in to kiss her.

Delbert cleared his throat. "You guys realize that you're going to need me."

Could Delbert get any more annoying? "For what?" Julka asked.

"The second test. Your first planned event. Seems someone figured out that the kids here weren't going to trick or treat because of the snow, so they'll need some kind of open house, complete with candy and costumes. I'm told that you have to organize it pronto, with enough advertising that the kids can find you."

Julka turned inside Marshall's arms. "What? We don't celebrate Halloween."

"But everyone here does," Marshall said. "So they told me I needed to show how well I could plan something—and do it fast—and so I thought of this."

"And then they told me that you'd need S-Elf assistance, so I'm going to assist," Delbert said, straightening up proudly.

Julka thought it all through. It only took a moment, but she realized what had just happened. She had gotten her Christmas wish. Wishes, actually. The ones she never talked about.

The ability to stay in the Greater World if she wanted. The chance to do a job she would love—organizing. And someone beside her. Someone who would love her and cherish her. Someone she would love and cherish.

"Delbert," she said. "We need some privacy."

"Then I suggest you leave here," Delbert said. "They can turn on the monitors any time."

Marshall slid his hand along her back and said softly, "My house is right outside."

"And besides," Delbert said loudly, as if he didn't want to hear any of that. "I have to find a great venue, and that'll take the sleigh. So get out."

They didn't have to be told twice. Julka took Marshall's hand and led him out of the sleigh. They barely made it down the steps when the sleigh took off, displacing the snow, and sending a huge greasy waft of peppermint-colored exhaust into the air.

"Is that normal?" Marshall asked, looking at the red-and-white smoke glistening around them.

"None of this is normal," Julka said.

"Oh, I don't know," Marshall said. "Men, women, kisses, soul mates. Seems normal enough to me."

He wrapped his arms around her again.

She giggled. "I thought you didn't believe in soul mates."

"I didn't believe in Santa either," he said. "Yet somehow, you managed to change my mind. In an instant. On both things."

Then he kissed her.

And kept kissing her as much as he could for the rest of their long, magical lives.

A GAME OF VIRGINS

LISA SILVERTHORNE

Acclaimed veteran fantasy and science fiction writer Lisa Silverthorne a wonderful dragon story full of heart and nifty takes on classic fantasy tropes. Really fun.

For a lot more about Lisa's stories and her growing new Game of Lost Souls series, go to http://www.lisasilverthorne.com/

A GAME OF VIRGINS

LISA SILVERTHORNE

Draven, a lesser emerald dragon stared at the screaming woman tied to a post outside the rocky cave where he'd been sleeping.

Another princess. He groaned. Too rich for him. Jewels and gold coins got stuck in his teeth. And virgins gave him reflux, especially loud, screeching princesses, but right now, he needed a virgin—some of her blood at any rate. To heal his wounds. They were severe and would take months to heal—if they healed.

The scratch of a dragon's claw across her left palm would tell him the truth. If it glowed, she was a virgin.

He had to find out.

Draven lifted his horned head, blowing ringlets of smoke into the cool spring breeze that swirled through the cave. How long had this rich, buttery princess roll-up on a stick (a favorite snack of most dragons) been out there? It hadn't been there when he arrived a day and a night ago.

Even from the depths of this dark cave, he'd smelled her

lilac perfume and buttery human scent above the smell of cave moss and loamy soil, heard her piercing screams and wailing. Her screaming would have attracted every dragon within a hundred miles of this cave.

Why hadn't one flown down already and picked her off in a single gulp?

Draven's stomach twisted into a knot. He'd have to hurry and save her from herself. And maybe she'd help him. He rubbed his head with a leathery green paw. Her screams were giving him a migraine on top of his other injuries.

A large company of knights ambushed him near a creek, trying to kill him for his scales. To make armor. He defeated the knights, but one wing and leg were badly injured. And a broken sword was still wedged tightly beneath his scales. Barely able to fly, he'd found this cave, hoping to crawl into its dark depths and heal.

A male voice rose above the screams. Draven froze. More humans! He was in no condition to fight anything.

A white-haired man with a gold crown, purple cape draped over one shoulder of his polished silver armor, stood beside the post where the princess had been tied. About three hundred feet or so away from the cave. The king was flanked by dozens of armored knights that stood on the dirt path winding down the hill and in the grass. In front of the post stood a row of barefoot women in flowing white gowns, wreaths of flowers on their heads. Dressed just like the princess tied to the post, except she wore a silver crown. Tears ran down their faces as they glanced from the cave to the princess tied to the post. She was quiet now, brown hair whipping in the wind, tangling into the folds of her diaphanous white gown.

"Here, you foul beast!" the white-haired king shouted and kicked open the lid of a battered wooden trunk that had been set at his feet. "Here is your tribute. Gathered by Prince Genaro betrothed to marry my only daughter. Who will never see her wedding day thanks to you. Now, leave our village in peace and may you burn in hell!"

Jewels and gold coins glimmered in the wash of sunlight, the trunk almost overflowing.

A young knight in shiny gold armor stepped up to the king's elbow. A fringe of light brown hair peeked out from his helmet and framed his oval face and light green-grey eyes. A sword perched on his left hip. His face was thin, nose sculpted perfection, jaw line strong, frame lean and lightly muscled. He kicked open a second chest of coins and jewelry.

"And here is Princess Emelina's bride price," he said, his smooth, velvety voice tight with anger. He gritted his teeth. "Paid in tribute to a dragon instead of her family. We were to be married. Rot in hell, you monster!"

Draven watched as the procession left the sobbing princess tied to the post and disappeared down the hillside path. He was relieved that they'd stopped lobbing princesses at the cave.

Well, this was awkward.

Draven unfurled his graceful, studded emerald wings and stretched. The cool darkness soothed his aching wing, but the sword lodged under his burnished green scales throbbed. He'd tried to remove it, but couldn't. He couldn't fly like this and he wanted no part of this tribute game the major and greater dragons played.

Just a little virgin blood and he'd be on his way.

He shifted his lean, leathery green body to the right in the dark cave, looking for the path out. He just missed knocking over a pile of broken skulls and bones. He turned left, squeezing around another pile of charred armor, but found only rock wall in his way.

The only way out was up. He sighed. To the cave's entrance. He had no choice but to go out that way. And get out of here before the huge dragon that had demanded tribute returned and killed him, too. But maybe, if he freed the princess, she'd reward him with a little blood to heal his wounds?

Piles of rusted metal and bones were strewn everywhere inside and outside this cave. Draven struggled around them. With so much debris lying around, whatever dragon lived in this cave had dwelled here a long, long time.

Draven had only seen one or two major dragons in his life-time. Bright scales of polished silver, bright copper, or brilliant gold. With a massive wingspan, wings dotted with rows of graduated sharp spikes that outlined its wings and rose in jagged peaks along its spine. Spitting fire and ice—and magic. Could shift form. And take out a thousand or more knights at once.

Uninjured, he could only fell about a hundred or so knights. He was young and lean with a lot of growing left to do (if his injuries healed). He stepped over another pile of rusted armor and stopped just short of the entrance.

Something about this cave felt—off.

Dragons marked their caves as a sign to other dragons. The symbol, two swirls with a line between them, meant home in the dragon language. They scratched through the symbol when they left. Draven hadn't found any such mark inside or outside this cave.

Besides, each dragon had its own sense of order, a place to eat, a bed of straw and cloth to sleep on, and a place for treasures, but this den lacked any structure. Everything seemed to be haphazardly strewn about. It was chaos!

No dragon had slept here recently besides him. He'd have smelled their scent. So where was this dragon that had demanded tribute from the neighboring village? Most dragons didn't bother humans—except the occasional raiding of their cattle or sheep. Dragons kept to themselves (like him), until stupid humans obsessed with their pointy sticks showed up to poke creatures ten times their size until they hit back. And then they cried about it until the entire countryside gathered to hunt it down and kill it.

Draven winced, the princess' wailing like claws against slate. He wouldn't be here for that part of the fun.

He put most of his weight on his right foot, the left one swollen and painful, its talons blunted. And knocked over a pile of rusting swords. One slid down a heap of charred, smashed armor and clanged against a blackened helmet. The helmet rolled over his left foot.

He howled in pain, stumbling backward. He couldn't fly. And he didn't want to mete out some old-fashioned fairy tale justice. He just wanted to lie in the sun. But he was a big bad dragon, blamed for swallowing up dozens of virgin princesses and noble knights.

But only in self-defense.

Stupid humans. He'd have to fight his way off the hillside. It would be some time before he could fly.

With a grunt, Draven swept his massive spiked tail across the cave's rocky floor, pushing the bones and debris against the wall. Stacks of broken swords, skeletons, and bloodied armor skittered across the dirt and thundered against the cave walls.

"Hmmm, wonder if I could recycle any of those?"

Had to make room to fight when the steady stream of lanky, knock-kneed man-children stumbling over their bravado and swords came to save the virgin princess. That they tied to a post and left without even a goodbye.

And he was tired of Princess Roll-up's shrill, screaming harpy voice.

He shuffled forward, but something blocked his path. Something rectangular and heavy. Draven reached out. Felt like a box or a chest of some kind.

Tilting his head up, Draven breathed an arc of fire across the chamber. There in the dark glistened five iron chests. Filled with gold coins, jewels, gold bars, and all types of jewelry, even crowns.

A fortune of riches! A major dragon's hoarded treasure? Or something else. Where did all of it come from—and why was it in here?

"Did you hear me, you horrid piece of luggage?" the princess' squeaky, high voice penetrated his sinuses. "Just you wait until my brave betrothed prince storms up that path to kill you!" She bared her pearly white teeth. "I'll mount your head on my throne room wall."

Time to leave. Before things got any worse.

Draven stepped out of the cave's darkness and into the warm sunlight.

The brown-haired princess' brown eyes bulged out as the wind fluttered through the folds of her white gown. Her mouth fell open and she let out the shrillest, sharpest screech he'd ever heard. The note almost pierced his ear drums.

"By the gods! No! NO!"

The knights in that castle below could probably hear her from the gates now. No wonder the village had been so eager to offer this one up as a sacrifice.

The princess fought the ropes binding her to the post, eyes brimming with tears, mouth open wide, chin bobbing.

"Help! Help, please!" she shouted. "This cave was empty! There weren't any dragons—it was abandoned!"

Footsteps crunched against rocks along the winding path that ran up the grassy hillside to the cave and down to a burbling creek below. From the creek, the hillside path weaved through the tall, wispy green grasslands to the gates of a stone castle.

At the top of the path stood Prince Genaro, the knight that had brought the bride price.

"My dear, Emelina," said the young man. He moved with cautious steps toward the post, his gaze flicking from Draven to the princess. "I've come to save you."

The look on the young man's face was strange, puzzling. Draven watched him with interest because he made no move to draw his sword.

"Genaro! Save me—please! Slay it!"

"Who me?" Draven said, shrugging at the knight. "I didn't demand a tribute. I was just here taking a nap."

"I assembled the tribute and the bride price just as you and your father asked." Genaro shook his head. "Just as Prince Relan did in HighKeep. And Prince Philippe from the Narrows. It seems that all three of us have been betrothed to the same princess. Emelina. Who has apparently been eaten by at least three dragons so far."

"What?" Princess Emelina stared at him, her eyes wide. "You know uh...Relan and Philippe?"

Genaro nodded. "That's why I came here to court you, Emelina. And then the most horrid thing happened. *Another* dragon demanded a virgin and riches as tribute. Right here." He pointed at the cave. "In this very cave. The same exact thing that happened to Relan and Philippe and others. So, I've waited, watching to see what would happen. Then this dragon appeared. Now, I'm confused."

Draven sighed. Time to speak up.

He unfurled his wings in a show of force. Pain snaked down his right side as he rose on his haunches and blew a burst of flame down the crag's dirt path.

The prince dropped to his knees, shielding his face as brush caught fire, crackling with smoke. A seedling fell on its side, charred and smoking.

The hilt under Draven's scales dug into his flesh again and he winced, letting his wings droop against his spine. Trying his best to hide his injuries.

"See why we must kill it," the princess snapped. "And now, my hair's going to be all frizzy, you big, stupid lizard! You're going to be so sorry when Genaro kills you!"

Draven turned toward the prince as he got to his feet, sword raised. "Look, I don't know who's playing whom here, but I know one thing for certain. I'm the only dragon to step out of this lair in a very long time. And I did not ask for tribute."

"A dragon with good grammar," said Genaro. "I'm impressed."

"Slay him, Genaro!" Princess Emelina shouted. "Slay him now!"

148

"She probably had people in the cave rattling bones and making noises to make you and the others think she was in danger," said Draven. "Besides, dragons mark their caves with a symbol in the dragon language. This one bears no mark. Oh, and one more thing."

Draven moved toward the post. He lifted his right paw and ran a sharp talon across the princess' left palm. Just hard enough to scratch.

Emelina screamed. "What are you doing? Genaro! Slay it before it kills me!"

Genaro watched as Draven stepped away from the post and pointed at the scratch on Emelina's palm. He waited several moments.

The scratch didn't glow.

"Afraid she isn't a virgin either," said Draven, turning back to Genaro. "You've been conned, prince."

"What?" Emelina's face turned beet red. "That's a lie! Genaro, please!"

Genaro's eyes darkened with anger as Draven cut the ropes binding the princess to the wooden post. She collapsed on the ground beside Genaro.

"From the looks of that cave, you've played this game several times, haven't you, princess," said Draven.

Genaro's grey-green eyes burned with fury. He stormed past Draven and stepped into the cave. A short time later, he returned, shaking his head.

"There's enough gold and jewels in there to fill every kingdom's treasury in a thousand miles," said Genaro. "Thanks, dragon. You've saved a lot of treasuries. And a few hearts to boot."

The princess stomped her foot, arms crossed, glaring at

Draven. "What? Why, I have never been so insulted in my entire life! You'll take a despicable dragon's word over mine?"

The prince whistled and several knights rushed up the hill.

"Take this—princess away. I'll assemble delegations from HighKeep, the Narrows, and Stormlake Falls. We'll discuss how to return this wealth."

A bloodcurdling screech echoed across the hillside, a huge shadow passing overhead. Fierce beat of wings.

Draven looked up. A huge silver dragon soared overhead. A greater dragon! It swooped across the dirt path, shouting at Draven in dragon's tongue.

"Nice gathering of wealth, little dragon," it said with a sharp hiss, circling the hillside. "You won't mind if I take it for myself in exchange for not killing you."

Draven groaned. He was too weak to fight. And he couldn't fly with an injured wing. Even on his best day, he was no match for a major dragon!

"I'll just snack on the humans while you decide."

A blast of icy air buffeted the hillside as the dragon swooped low. Its tail swept the hilltop, knocking Draven, Genaro, Emelina, and the knights to the ground.

"Into the cave!" Draven shouted. "Hurry!"

Everyone got to their feet and darted toward the cave. Draven waited until the last human was in front of him before he limped forward. When the dragon dived toward Genaro, Draven unleashed a fury of fiery breath at it.

The dragon screeched, its left wing on fire. It puffed cold breath onto its wing until it extinguished the fire.

"Why do you defend them?" the dragon shouted, enraged by Draven's attack.

"Because I'm tired of greed," Draven yelled. "On both sides."

The major dragon circled the hilltop again, dropping down in front of the cave's entrance.

Draven stretched his wings as wide as he could, the pain excruciating, and blocked the major dragon's path.

"When I engage him," Draven said to the humans behind him, "All of you run down the path. I can't save your riches, but I can get you safely down the hillside."

"That massive dragon will kill you," said Genaro, shaking his head. "Why are you—?"

"Go!" Draven shouted.

Draven lifted his emerald snout and spat a huge fireball at the big dragon. It screeched, skittering backward as Genaro, Emelina, and the knights bolted out of the cave. Draven rushed forward and leaped at the major dragon, talons extended, and shot a stream of fire into the dragon's face.

They tumbled backward, rolling across the dirt and grass, screeching and shooting ice and fire.

Draven collapsed, the major dragon standing over him.

"Say goodnight, little dragon," said the silver dragon, hissing a bolt of ice at Draven.

He rolled left, the magic missing him as the major dragon rose up on its haunches and plunged its talons deep into Draven's leathery hindquarters, slipping past scales. Gouging deep.

Draven let out a cry of pain and kicked out, catching the major dragon's snout as it freed its talons. Lifting them toward Draven's throat.

A hail of arrows hit the major dragon. It swung its tail, knocking away a handful of knights as Genaro leaped forward, sliding underneath. His blade sliced into the major dragon's tail and it shrieked, flailing.

Talons raised, the major dragon turned.

A rush of wind and darkness swept across the hillside and slammed into the major dragon.

Another major dragon! Its scales were polished onyx, spikes long and sharp as it locked horns with the major dragon, both tumbling down the dirt path.

"Dragon, this way," said Genaro, tugging on his good wing.

Prince Genaro and the knights helped Draven down the dirt path and into the scraggly forest below. Just over a rise, where the creek bend curved away toward a stand of evergreens stood a small cave in the side of a grassy slope. Draven crawled into the cool, dark chamber, chest heaving, sticky black dragon's blood oozing across wing and haunch.

Genaro dropped down on Draven's left side. "This wound is so deep," said the prince as he pulled off his gloves. "I've got to stop the bleeding. I need bandages."

Draven nodded. It cut to the bone. A mortal blow. At least, he'd done one good thing in saving this prince and his knights. Maybe these humans would tell the story and not think that all dragons were evil.

"This will work."

"Hey!" Emelina shouted as Genaro tore off a piece of her white gown.

"You saved our lives back there," said Genaro, pressing the cloth against the wound. "Why?"

"You were no match for that dragon." His chest was heavy. Getting hard to breathe. "It—wasn't a fair fight."

Genaro yelped, pulling his hand back.

"Those talons are sharp," Genaro muttered, holding his left hand.

The prince's face turned red as his left palm began to glow. He stared at Draven.

Draven motioned toward him. "Just a little bit of your blood can heal me."

At last, Genaro nodded. He ran his palm across the sharp talon. Hard. Wincing, as blood ran down his wrist. He reached out and pressed his bloody hand to the jagged wound in Draven's hindquarters.

Pale gold light traveled down the stream of blood, encircling his wrist and running across Draven's emerald scales. Settling into the wound. In moments, the gold light encased his entire body from talons to wing tips, a soft thrumming sound reverberating in Draven's ears.

His fire magic began to pulse and hum, building into a bright burst of magic that exploded through the cave. And everything went dark.

After a few moments, someone lit a torch.

"By the gods! What happened?" one of the knights shouted.

Draven felt strange, his body still humming with magic. He felt...smaller somehow. Different.

He sat up. Staring at Genaro. Eye to eye.

"You're human!" Genaro shouted.

Draven looked at his soft, fleshy hands and arms. He reached up and felt thick bushy hair on his head. At his ears. That burst of healing had boosted his own fire magic, teaching him to shift form. Something only mature dragons could do.

Genaro grinned at him, extending his hand. Draven reached out and shook it.

"Dragons can shift form," said Draven. "I hadn't expected to learn that until I was at least a hundred." The distant screech of a dragon made Draven freeze. "Your blood healed me, but I'm still no match for a major dragon." He chuckled. "Or two. We'd better wait until they've fought it out and gone. Then you can salvage anything that's left for your other Keeps."

Genaro nodded. "Y'know, Emelina isn't the only princess playing the virgin game out there. Giving dragons a bad name and all. With your newfound form, you'd be a big help taking the others down. And a great bodyguard for a prince. Interested?"

Draven smiled. "I am. And by the way, I wouldn't have eaten that princess or any other human. I don't eat meat."

Genaro's mouth fell open. "A vegetarian dragon?"

"A virgin prince?" Draven replied.

"Okay, you win," said Genaro, still blushing.

Draven leaned back against the wall, watching Genaro and the other humans with newfound interest. He liked this new game much better than the other one.

SOUL MATE JUNKIE AND THE BEATING HEART

DAVID H. HENDRICKSON

David H. Hendrickson, with this story, did one of the most powerful sf stories I have read in some time. Original and yet familiar at the same time. I can't say any more for fear of spoiling it.

Just hang on.

His short fiction has appeared in Best American Mystery Stories 2018, Ellery Queen's Mystery Magazine, Heart's Kiss, *and numerous anthologies, including over a half dozen issues of* Fiction River *and just about every issue of this magazine so far. Check it all out at http://www.hendricksonwriter.com/*

SOUL MATE JUNKIE AND THE BEATING HEART

DAVID H. HENDRICKSON

Emily Jones, her shoulders slumped and eyes bloodshot, swiped her badge at the entrance of the crumbling, three-story, red brick building. Located on the banks of the Merrimack River in an impoverished, old mill town north of Boston, the building stood as tall as it was wide and deep, a hundred fifty feet of grime in each direction. A black smoke-stack on the far left near the back fouled the air with a dank, musky odor.

Outside, no sign announced the business's name, though cars filled the side parking lot. Inside the windowless, anti-septic foyer that ran the full width of the building but extended only fifteen feet deep, a sign in old English script with exaggerated curlicues read, *La fabrique d'amour.*

The Love Factory.

As if spelling it out in French made what Emily and all the others did in this dungeon suddenly romantic and exciting. A sour taste filled Emily's mouth. She swiped her credit card-sized badge across the scanner beside the middle of five heavy metal doors, and after the beep, pulled it open. As she walked past the side stairwell and its surveillance camera, then down the cavernous, concrete-walled corridor, the door clanged shut behind her, sounding like the closing of a door to a prison cell.

Another day of her sentence.

Twenty-nine years old, she felt like seventy-nine. No beauty, but not physically repulsive either, Emily had limp, shoulder-length, auburn hair, a pug nose that she knew cried out for cosmetic surgery, a flat chest that cried out even more, and an extra twenty-five pounds she'd been trying unsuccessfully to rid herself of for all her adult life. Most noticeable of all, though, she looked worn out and used up, her brown eyes vacant and downcast, her lips grim and never smiling.

No wonder Mark was thinking of leaving her. Probably more than just thinking, too. It had to be a lead-pipe certainty.

But he was supposed to be *the one*. They were supposed to be *soul mates*. Like John and Kevin and Jason and Tom and Jared and Ryan before Mark. Now, like all those before him, Mark was growing distant. Cold.

Even though she'd crossed the line she swore she'd never cross. Emily had become not just an employee, but a customer.

Her footfalls echoed down the corridor, as did those of five or six other faceless employees, until she stopped in front of the door to unit 349A. She swiped her badge across yet another scanner, and stepped inside what she'd come to think of as her tomb. It was a thin sliver of a room, the air heavy and humid. More closet than room, really. Though barely more than five feet tall, Emily could hold out her arms and simultaneously touch both side walls. The far wall stood less than ten feet from the door. The ceiling only seven feet high. Its barren walls painted industrial green, "the tomb" smelled faintly of mildew and Lysol at the same.

It held only one thing: the chamber. When she had first come to work there, she had thought it looked like a tanning bed. Slide in and pull down the lid, though she did so fully clothed. Now, though, she thought of it as a coffin.

Emily slid into the chamber, pushed her badge into the slot in the lid above her, and pulled the lid down. Her balance glowed on the screen above her.

0.00

And that was after the emergency withdrawal from her bank account to rectify yesterday's negative balance after too many purchases of the company's products. A bank account that was now as dry and empty as she was, with no more funds to cover any emergency, no matter how dire.

Even if it was the difference between Mark leaving her or not.

So it was time to get to work. Again. Too many hours because of too many purchases. Emily's fingers itched and her mouth felt dry. Deep inside her chest, her heart ached. She wanted to cry even though it wasn't yet time for that.

Swallowing hard, Emily touched her fingertips to the recessed sensors on both sides of her. She began to read from the built-in screen on the lid. In no time, her fingertips tingled, and the air smelled of ozone. Tears streamed down the sides of her face, blurring the words on the screen until she blinked the tears away. Emily devoured the words and emitted her premium-cut emotions into the fingertip sensors.

She began to cry. Her sobs grew louder and more forceful until her entire body shook, wracked with their pain. Even so, she held her fingertips to the sensors, never losing contact.

The consummate professional.

At the beginning, it had been her dream job. Get paid to read romance novels. She already did that for free! What was the catch? Compared to her previous position as a social worker—having her heart ripped out on a daily basis and then having to come back the next day to do it all over again—the position of Senior Emotopath felt like stealing the company's money.

It was *so* easy. Like the proverbial taking candy from babies. During her job interview she scored highly—off the charts, actually—in the company's "emotion emission" scores.

Emily *oozed* emotion. It poured out of her like sweat from a fat man in a sauna. She was hired on the spot as a Senior Emotopath. No junior designation. No probationary period. No references. Can you start now?

"Today?" she had asked.

"Now!"

She needed no mentor or training. Emily was a natural.

She hit all her quotas and then kept going, accumulating bonus after bonus. The company drew off her "premium-level" emotion emissions, distilled and matured them in the emoto-vats that filled the entire basement floor below, then added them to its products. Emily's exported emotions, as well as those of the other Emotopaths, were the key ingredient in the company's Soul Mates Series of couple's jewelry, guaranteed to draw both partners closer together than ever—make them true soul mates, the one and only for each other—as well as the potent essence in the Soul Mates perfume and cologne lines, designed to attract a soul mate to the lonely wearer of the scent.

According to the company-sponsored research, the products worked. They were no late-night infomercial gimmicks. There was no placebo effect. *They worked!*

Not all the time, of course. There had to be *some* element of destiny involved. Otherwise, what was the point. One couldn't *totally* manufacture the pure joy of being soul mates. No Emotopath emissions—even Emily's supercharged ones, no matter how distilled and matured—could turn Joan of Arc and Attila the Hun into soul mates.

You couldn't just bathe in Soul Mates bubble bath or splash on Soul Mates perfume or cologne and then automatically ensnare the object of your desire. Gotcha! Never going to let you go.

There was always free will and the element of chance. But the jewelry, perfumes, colognes, and the rest of the product line could help when that little something extra was needed.

Like with Mark.

And so Emily had bought them matching Soul Mates watchbands. And they had become immediately closer. More intimate in every way.

When that began to wear off, she'd bought them the special couple's version of Soul Mates perfume and cologne, designed not to attract someone new but to maintain and strengthen a pre-existing bond.

And that at least *seemed* to work. For a while.

But when even that effect flickered, when she'd eventually gone through the entire company catalog, working countless overtime hours to pay for it all, she resorted to a secret benefit available only to employees, though not one that would ever appear in a corporate Human Resources handbook.

Who, Emily asked herself, could ever put a price on true love?

After pouring all of her emotions into the fingertip sensors, she checked on her balance, entered the secret code, and withdrew the entire balance on as much of the pure stuff as her money could buy.

The purest of the pure. Uncut. As far from the watered down, commercially available Soul Mate products as the purest heroin in Afghanistan was to the stomped-on, diluted imitator being sold four blocks away from the factory.

Emily let it pour over her. It would make her irresistibly attractive to Mark, bind them together like never before. Forever and ever.

Soul Mates at last.

She could feel his presence atop her in the chamber. He wasn't actually there, of course; there wasn't enough room for a couple inside the chamber no matter how petite they might both be, and Mark was almost six feet tall and two hundred pounds.

But she felt his presence nonetheless. Smelled the spicy cinnamon fragrance of his Soul Mates cologne. Tasted the minty taste of Soul Mates mouthwash on his lips. Felt his facial hair brush pleasantly against her cheeks.

In her mind, Emily wrapped her arms around him. Held him close. Closer. And closer still. She felt his weight pressing upon her in the most pleasurable of places.

They were meant for each other. Nothing could tear them asunder.

Soul Mates forever.

E mily had never before tested the limits of her badge's access, but she was desperate now. Beyond desperate.

When she had returned to the small, studio apartment she and Mark shared following her immersion in the Soul Mate purest of the pure, she had wrapped her arms around him every bit as tightly as she had imagined in the chamber and they had made love feverishly for their longest time ever. They hadn't just rutted like animals. They had…

Made.

Love.

Like only true soul mates could do.

And then they had enjoyed a wonderful dinner of coconut shrimp, chicken-stuffed crepes, and brownies a la mode. They went for a long walk, hand in hand, her head resting on his shoulder. And come back to the apartment and made wonderful, soul-mate love all over again.

Just the way Emily had envisioned they would spend the rest of their lives.

But lying together in bed this morning, Mark had turned his face away when she went to kiss him—"For the love of God, could you brush your teeth first?" he'd begged—and then added, "And while you're at it, could you take a shower?"

As if his own breath didn't stink, and the dried-sweat remnants of their lovemaking weren't on him, too. Hell, his hair was sticking up every which way like a goddamn doofus. Your shit stinks, too, buddy.

But it wasn't the smell of his breath or their mutually dried, stale sweat that bothered Emily. It was that *it mattered*.

"For the love of God, could you brush your teeth first?"

and, "while you're at it, could you take a shower?" were not the pillow talk of soul mates.

What Emily knew she needed was a more potent or a longer-lasting, perhaps infinite supply of the pure stuff that had made last night so magical. Even if her bank account was empty and her work balance not a penny over 0.00.

She'd worked *so* many hours lately to pay for everything. She felt so drained of energy, particularly emoto-energy, she doubted she could conjure up much of a balance lying there in her chamber. And whatever balance she could manage, it would be only the smallest fraction of what she needed right now. Needed to restore last night's bliss of her relationship with Mark.

And dammit, didn't she *deserve* it? Not just the result—the bliss of a soul-mate relationship—but the product, too. Didn't she deserve the purest of the pure, uncut emoto-essence. Should she really have had to pay so dearly the day before? Wasn't her essence the most premium of them all? She had no idea how the company distilled and matured it, transforming her raw essence into a finished product, but they were gauging her just to get back a piece of herself!

It wasn't fair.

If she didn't have the funds to buy back her own essence in distilled and finished form—and she most certainly didn't—then maybe she should just *take it*. Take back what was hers to begin with! Or maybe she could even form an alliance with others who needed the primo product as much as she did? Convince the company to do right by them and give them back a piece of themselves for free.

Emily thought of the drawn faces and haggard looks of her fellow Emotopaths, most of them women but a few of them men, always looking down as they walked to their chambers, never wasting an emotion on a co-worker, on a fellow traveler on this road to nowhere. Were all of them as dependent—as desperate for love eternal in the form of soul mates—as she was?

Not that she was actually desperate, of course. Emily thought, though, that the rest of them probably were. But would they be of any help in getting what they so dearly required? Or would they just get in the way?

Or would there not be enough to go around? Might she have to share a little too much and not be left enough to give her and Mark their happily ever after?

Emily decided to go it alone.

———

I t took three skin-crawling days before Emily got her chance. A red-headed woman she did not recognize, bright-eyed and bushy-tailed with broad shoulders, muscular arms—a new hire?—was entering the building at the same time as Emily. Big Red, as Emily instantly nicknamed her, swiped her badge to enter the stairwell and headed down the circular stairs. Emily caught the door just before it closed and ducked inside. Company policy, of course, strictly forbade tailgating, but Emily figured company policy also forbade employees stealing back what was rightfully theirs.

She followed Big Red down the winding metal steps, their footfalls echoing in the claustrophobic air until they reached the heavy metal door to the basement floor. Big Red swiped her badge against the sensor, and stepped inside.

Emily followed.

Big Red frowned. "You work here?"

Emily nodded. "Transferred."

Big Red nodded, then headed down the long corridor with Emily in her wake. The corridor was as cavernous as the one upstairs, but it looked like there were only doors on the right side.

"Where you headed?" Big Red asked.

That was the million dollar question, wasn't it? Emily mustered as nonchalant and confident of a look as she could manage and said, "Emoto-vat."

Big Red nodded, but then gave a quizzical look. "We went past the door." She pointed to the lone door on the left twenty-feet behind them. Not knowing it was there, Emily had missed it.

"Yeah, right," Emily said, then headed back to the vat door. She felt Big Red's eyes on her back, but what could she do?

As Emily had feared, a scanner hung waist-high to the right of the emoto-vat door. Her badge most certainly was not programmed to provide access. In fact, it almost certainly would set off alarms. What had ever come over her, thinking she could come down here and get away with it? Now, she'd almost certainly get fired, and then where would that leave her and Mark? Emily drew in a deep breath and tried to calm her nerves.

"Could you swipe me in?" Emily said, improvising as best as she could. She held up her badge, showing her headshot and name. "I'm Emily Jones, and I'm supposed to check on one of the vats, but they messed up the reprogramming of my badge. You know. With the transfer and all."

Big Red stared at Emily, and cocked her head to the side.

Emily waved the badge and pointed to the photo. "Emily Jones. See. I was working on the first floor."

"An Emotopath?" Big Red asked.

"One of the best," Emily said, finally telling the truth about something. "Senior Emotopath." Silence hung in the heavy air. Emily added, "They wanted me to see the entire operation. I think they have big plans for me." She grinned. "Although they probably won't give me a raise."

Big Red nodded thoughtfully, and after hesitating a few more seconds, she swiped her badge across the scanner. The heavy metal door opened, and Emily stepped inside the vast room. From left to right, it spanned the entire building's one hundred and fifty feet, and was about sixty feet deep. Floor-to-near-ceiling metal vats ran along each wall, side-by-side, with rubber tubing the size of fire hoses attached to the bottom and top of each. Electrical wiring entered the top of each vat. The smell of ozone filled the air.

Emily stood frozen. Like the proverbial dog who chases a car with no idea of what to do once he catches it, Emily had no idea what to do next.

Although the hoses certainly looked inviting.

"You're not supposed to be here, are you?" Big Red said.

Emily opened her mouth, unsure of what to say, and then told the truth.

"My boyfriend and I," she began, "we need more of the good stuff than we can afford. He's my soul mate. I just know it. We get *so close* to each other, but then it wears off." Emily licked her dry lips. "But look at all of this! I don't know what's what, but this is enough for a lifetime. For both of us and both our lovers! Enough to keep an army of Emotopaths and you going for life. Without getting bled dry by the company."

But Big Red was backing away, eyes wide, shaking her head. And then she was gone out the door.

Alarm sirens shattered the silence.

———

F iguring she had nothing more to lose, Emily sprinted to the nearest vat, leaped up and grabbed hold of the hose above her head. It pulled loose and Emily tumbled to the hard concrete floor. She looked up expectantly as red alarms strobed the air and sirens blared, but....

Nothing. Not a drop came from the exposed hose.

She ran to another vat, leaped up to grab another hose and...

A trickle of something moist dropped onto her face, but...

Emily felt nothing. For a few moments, at least.

Then, the floor began to shift beneath her feet. She didn't know what it represented, but it sure didn't equate to eternal soul mate status for her and Mark. Suddenly, it registered to her that the upper hoses had to be intake hoses filling the emoto-vat and the lower ones outtake, draining it.

Emily dropped to her knees and wrestled the nearest lower hose loose. A viscous dark fluid washed over her. Images of her and Mark flooded her mind. Walking along the beach, hand in hand. Kissing each other passionately. Her walking up the aisle of a church while an organ played "Here Comes the Bride," and Mark watched adoringly, clad in a black tuxedo.

The purest of the pure. This was it.

Emily laid down on the cold concrete and let it pour over her. She closed her eyes and wrapped her arms around her thoughts of Mark.

————

I t was sheer bliss. Emily didn't hear the sirens blare
anymore or see the red alarm strobe lights. All she saw
was her and Mark, together forever. The greatest of all soul
mates.

Until the floor lifted her up. *You can't stay here.*

The viscous black fluid poured onto the floor, flooding it.
Emily floated atop the fluid. Then atop a cushion of air atop
the fluid.

Got to get you out.

Emily rolled over, splashing in the fluid, splashing it all
over her face, arms, and legs, but then felt herself lifted up
above it again.

*This place is killing you. You have to get out and never come
back.*

Emily screamed. Get out and never come back? Never! She
smeared the fluid over her face, and over her breasts, and over
her thighs. As she did, she felt Mark's loving hands doing the
smearing, lingering lovingly on her breasts and thighs, then
kissing her.

Taking you out of here.

"No!" Emily screamed.

She stumbled to her feet, fell, then crawled to the vat still
spewing the fluid. Emily ducked her head in the flow and let it
cascade over her until it ran dry. The fluid covered the floor,
inches deep.

Get out! Get away from here!

But Emily wasn't going away. Not now. Not ever. She felt
wonderful.

She stumbled to the next vat, and yanked loose the hose.

And the next and the next. Let it all spill out.

Got to get you out!

Emily lay in the fluid, arms spread wide, beseeching Mark to join her. Come to me my love. Come, my darling.

The fluid rose until it covered her chin, then her lips, and then almost her nose.

Got to save you. For your own good. Before it's too late.

The floor pulsed, lifting Emily up from the fluid, then dropping her back down again. And then it pulsed again.

As if finding its rhythm, the floor spasmed over and over, lifting Emily up and then down, slowly carrying her out the emoto-vat room's door.

"Let me go!" Emily cried. She got to her knees, but again the floor contracted and expanded, knocking her down, moving her down the corridor, toward the stairwell.

"No! You can't take this away from me!" she screamed, as Big Red and two other women raced passed her and disappeared into the stairwell.

The corridor walls joined the floor and ceiling, contracting and expanding, pulsing furiously. As Emily fought them, they blew the door off the stairwell.

Contracting and expanding, beating like a heart, they pushed Emily up the stairs with blasts of billowing air even as she fought to get back to the vats, the precious vats, and what they held for her and Mark.

"I've got to have it!"

Forget about Mark! Forget about soul mates!

The words—the blasphemy—turned Emily's blood cold. Shivers ran up and down her spine. Maybe, just maybe, Mark wasn't *the one*. If she couldn't get back and flood herself with more of that purest of pure Soul Mate essence—and more

172

importantly cover *him* with the essence—then perhaps he was a lost cause. Mark might not be her soul mate after all.

But she would never ever, ever, ever forget about finding her true soul mate. She would find him if it was the last thing she did. It was what gave her life meaning.

Forget about soul mates? Who would say such a horrible thing?

Somehow, Emily knew it was *the building* speaking such a blasphemy. It was *the factory*, perhaps a slaughterhouse or a tannery in decades long past, and it held deep within itself the stains of blood and guts spilled long before she was even born.

It was this factory—*La fabrique d'amour*—that was trying to take away from her everything she cared about. She would never stop searching for her soul mate. Never!

You will or it will ruin you.

The pocket of air pulsed and pulsed, stronger and stronger, carrying her up to the first floor even as her arms flailed for purchase. It blew out the door and blew her out into the lobby.

Then it blew out all the doors. And blew her, tumbling, out the front door and onto the crumbling, weed-strewn sidewalk. The building contracted and expanded, ejecting one prisoner after another.

"I want it back!" Emily cried, thinking desperately of the black, viscous fluid that was the missing secret to her happiness.

You can't have it back. All of this was killing you.

Emily stared in disbelief as the building, its grimy, crumbling red brick exterior contracted and expanded like a beating heart.

Thump-thump, thump-thump.

Ejecting on a cushion of air one woman after another, and

173

then an occasional man. Out the front doors. A crowd of them spilled onto the empty street and the side parking lot.

Thump-thump, thump-thump.

Emily ran crying for the front door, desperate to get back in and feel that viscous fluid pour over her again, make her feel *alive* and *in love* again. But the pulsating wind buffeted her, pushing her back, back, back. Giving her no more control of her body than if she were being carried by a tornado.

Thump-thump, thump-thump.

The crowd of employees stared in horror as the factory pulsed, spewing broken red bricks through the air.

It beat faster and faster, jackhammering with increasing force.

Thump-thump, thump-thump. Thump-thump, thump-thump.

Faster and faster still until finally, it ejected one last factory employee. One last prisoner.

You all are safe, now, the factory seemed to say to Emily. *You need be enslaved no longer.*

Emily knew she had been enslaved. A soul mate junkie. But she also knew that as soon as she could go back into that damned factory, she would run as fast as her legs could carry her, and she would immerse herself in whatever remained of that sweet black, viscous fluid that told her that she and Mark could be soul mates forever more. Her life would have value, would have meaning. She would dive in the fluid and let it drown her, if need be.

Because it was all she had.

I will show you what true love really is. I will save you from yourself.

The heart of the building beat faster and faster, contracting more and more wildly. More crumpled bricks flew through the air as it spasmed and spasmed.

Faster and faster.

Until finally, the beating, brick heart collapsed in on itself, imploding with an ear-splitting crash, sending plumes of crumbled bricks up into the sky, and filling the air with their dry smoke.

La fabrique d'amour—The Love Factory—beat no more.

UNCOMFORTABLE SHOES

ROB VAGLE

Rob Vagle is a long-time professional writer who is becoming a regular contributor to Pulphouse, something I am very happy about. I feel lucky to have his work in the magazine.

His stories are all different and all powerful in a Pulphouse sort of way. In this original story Rob takes us to a shoeshine stand in an airport, in a way only Rob can do.

I suggest you go to https://robvagle.com/ to find out a lot more about his fantastic stories and books.

UNCOMFORTABLE SHOES

ROB VAGLE

Benjamin's shoeshine station smelled like a perfume counter in a departments store due to the crowd of travelers departing and arriving during morning travel in Concourse B.

His station was among the restaurants and eateries and news stands. The air was filled with the smell of cheap Teriyaki chicken and coffee. The carpet was a soothing blue with airplanes depicted throughout. The carpet cut down on the noise drummed up from feet walking up and down the concourse.

His display held a voluminous selection of Kiwi brand shoe supplies like tins of shoeshine, shoe laces, cloths, and brushes. He thought the Kiwi shoe polish smelled kind of like gasoline. He also had sundries like bottled water, snacks, mints, combs, sunglasses, hair brushes, hair nets, and newspapers. His father had recommended keeping the cigars because they were a big seller, and Benjamin was glad he had listened to his old man. The visitors to the shoeshine stand liked cigars over bottled water.

Down the concourse, towards the security gates, a cello and a piano were playing an upbeat tune. It carried well in the concourse and gave the place more of a museum feel than a travel hub.

Benjamin had been shining shoes in the airport for two years, after taking over for his father when he retired. He felt it lacked the glamour and importance of office work, all those poor workers in their cubicles seeing the same old faces every day.

Shining shoes didn't pay much but it was a business handed to him by his old man. Although he dreamt of selling the business and pursuing something that interested him more, like using his college English and Humanities degrees to do something for the greater good.

The truth was he didn't know what that something might be. English degrees were notoriously known to be useless, except for getting into teaching. His old man laughed at Benjamin for taking on an English degree saying that was as useless as a buggy whip for an automobile. Benjamin didn't like the thought of teaching, but he liked to keep an open mind.

Physical labor jobs never much interested him. Jobs like construction, groundskeeping, and custodial. He'd rather use his head, to read and think. He saved the physical for his favorite activities like Tae Kwon Do and running.

He hated the thought of restaurant or retail work because that would be dealing with the general public and that was fraught with assholes and jerks and other terrible people who wouldn't give you the time of day. They'd rather step on you then get around you.

Then here he was in a job that was not unlike retail. Because here he was dealing with the general public. He would give up this occupation at any time, but now this occupation was easy. It was a stopping point, like many of these airport travelers making a connecting flight. Just a stop before the journey continues.

And Benjamin had two things going for him in this airport as a shoeshine man.

One, it was exciting seeing people going somewhere and meeting world travelers, whether business men and women, or vagabonds seeing new and strange places. It wasn't like serving people their rice and bean bowls in the *Cafe Yumm* down at the other end of the concourse. Here, at the shoeshine stand, the traveler can take a breather and just sit still. They've already committed to a shine, so there was no selling. It was in those quiet moments, when they were talkative—and honestly they were more talkative than not—Benjamin could draw them out through conversations, listen to what they say, and see what they were made of.

The second thing, was a bigger thing. A strange thing. A thing nobody else was born with, it seemed, except for Benjamin. Some might call it a skill. Some might call it a curse. But what Benjamin had the knack to do was putting himself inside the shoes of anyone who needed a shine.

One could call it a psychic talent because Benjamin did see things, sometimes as soon as a customer sat in one of the three chairs on a raised platform against the wall. Other times it didn't happen until he touched the shoe.

When he touched the shoe he saw their past. He saw their

departure and their destination. Sometimes he could even save them with a warning. Perhaps by dispensing some unassuming wisdom.

He never knew if he saved anyone. It might be unlikely, but he never liked to think so. There was a paradox to all this. If he could save them with a bit of a warning or wisdom, then he shouldn't be seeing anything at all in his mind's eye when they sit down.

One time he had a vision (he didn't like the adjective *psychic*) with a business man from New York, probably worked in Wall Street. In his mind's eye Benjamin saw the man walking into an elevator, following a woman in a with long blond hair. It was just the two of them. She was staring up at the numbers above the door. He leered at her—he didn't see his face because he saw everything from his point of view, and felt it—and then he placed his hands around her neck and squeezed. She lets out a quick startled breath, before being cut off.

The image was so shocking and unexpected. He had no idea if it was in the past or future. Benjamin backed away from the man's two thousand dollar Italian leather shoes.

The man lowered The New York Times.

"I can't shine your shoes, sir," Benjamin said.

"Why?" the man asked.

They stared at each other for a quiet moment, Benjamin a loss for words. Honesty might get him punched or the his father's shoeshine stand might get a bad reputation—his son didn't have the knack with customers, they would say.

"Well?" the man asked, his brows curled low over his eyes and a scowl on his face.

Benjamin pointed at the sign on above the man's head. "We

have the right to refuse service to anyone. I don't have to tell you why."

The sign did give the proper disclosure.

The man grumbled and picked up his things. Pulled the handle for his pull along luggage and said, "You should pay me for wasting my time."

Then she stepped into his shoeshine stand.

She was traveling in a black dress that reached just above the knees. She was brunette with curls. On first impression, Benjamin assumed the woman was in her thirties, much older than he was and way out of his league. Brunette curls tumbled around her shoulders and down her back. Her shoulders and arms were bare and skin looked tanned to a healthy bronze.

Most of Benjamin's friends, the male ones, were surprised when they heard women stopped at his father's shoeshine stand. It may not happen frequently, but women did on occasion, whether for a shine or to fix a shoe malfunction, like a heel or torn strap. And it wasn't unheard of for a woman wanting a shine on their shoes.

In fact, his old man had been savvy—because why lose a potential revenue stream—and was known for providing a safe, comfortable environment for women clientele. A tradition Benjamin held onto. This included having a lower chair and a large bath towel she could cover her lap with. This was required if a woman was wearing a skirt or dress.

Like the woman who stepped into the shoeshine stand now.

She wasn't carrying any luggage, but she had a large handbag over her shoulder. Black just like the dress. Her eyes were blue with light mascara. Benjamin thought it was nicely done and he didn't realize his heart started pounding as he noticed these things. Her lips had a glistening coat of lipstick.

"Hi," she said as she sat on the middle chair, which was on the raised platform.

Benjamin reacted immediately and went to the drawer and pulled out a towel and handed it to her. It was cotton, thick and soft.

"Good morning," he said. "Put that in your lap. Unless you prefer the lower chair."

He pointed to the one at the end standing apart from the platform. It all came out natural and unassuming, just like his old man. Providing a woman's needs at the shoeshine stand required subtlety and grace.

"Oh my goodness," she said as she looked down at herself. "The towel would be appropriate. Thank you."

She sounded enthusiastic and sincere. She smelled sweet and flowery with a hint of perspiration and Benjamin thought she might have been on a red eye flight.

She wore blue shoes that matched her eyes. They were leather pumps with a one inch, thick heel.

"What can I do for you today, madam?" he asked.

She looked at him with a funny look and then laughed. "Madam, please! Call me Persephone."

It was Benjamin's turn to laugh. "Like the Greek goddess," he said.

"That's me. On a good day."

"Well, Persephone, what can I do for you?"

"Shine please," she said, wiggling her feet those blue shoes. "I want these babies to shine."

She had both feet up on the vinyl foot stool. When

Benjamin sat down and first touched them with the cloth, the vision was instantaneous.

In the vision she said to him: *I thought all shoeshiners were old guys.*

As he ran the cloth over the toe of her right shoe, she then said to him, live: "I thought all shoeshiners were old guys."

He looked up into her mesmerizing eyes and felt like he was in a spotlight of love. Her attention was all on him. He wanted to say he thought she would say that, but he couldn't get the words out. The fact he had had a vision and it became true in two seconds astounded him.

"I'm sorry. You're not an Uber driver. They always want to talk," she said.

"No, you're good," he said. "I hear that all the time. About shoeshiners being old guys. This my old man's business. Well, it's mine now and it's just a temporary occupation."

"You're not going to do this until your sixty-four," she said.

"No, ma'm," he said.

She nudged his hand with her left foot. "Persephone!"

Even though he had a split second to see her beam a smile at him, the nudge sent his mind plummeting through a vision, a series of visions. He and her sitting next to each other in a dark movie theater with explosions on the screen. He and her finishing swing dancing and clinging to one another. Her telling him it's been a great first year over dinner in small restaurant with only half dozen tables.

Then the last vision: her seeing him, Benjamin, in a casket. She was crying, her vision blurry with tears.

He tumbled back off his stool and landed on the carpet, his breath rushing out of him.

"Man overboard! Are you okay?" she asked.

He saw shoes pass before his eyes—loafers and some dude was wearing galoshes for some reason. Luggage were being pulled like children's wagons and anybody that looked down at him had uninterested looks on their faces. Didn't they know they were looking at a dead man?

"Are you hurt?" Persephone asked.

She was standing now. The towel from her lap had dropped onto her shoes. He hopped to his feet and shook himself, snapping the cloth out in his right hand.

He tried to recover—but how does one recover seeing themselves dead?—and said, "Happens sometimes. It's dangerous work."

"You're still standing," she said proudly. And she clapped her hands softly at him.

He bowed and said, "Now, Persephone, if you sit down we can get back down to business."

"Finish our little party," she said as she sat down.

Benjamin felt himself blush, his cheeks burning hot.

They were flirting with each other. They would date. And he would die.

How would he die?

He had to focus. Focus on shining her shoes. He couldn't contemplate his own corpse from her eyes. When he opened the tin of polish, the whiff of the gasoline-like smell cleared his head. He set to work on her pumps and let her talk.

From his use of the cloth to the horsehair brush on her blue pumps, Persephone talked. She had actually graduated from the same high school as he did, four years ahead of him. She went to college for business and now worked for The Bannon hotel chain. She had just come from Las Vegas where they just finalized a deal for a new hotel there.

While she talked Benjamin only muttered one word sentences, except for the part about her going to the same high school. On that point they both came up with names and faces, mostly teachers, they both knew.

Benjamin came away with one thought: she was much more together than he was. She was into her career and seemed to know where she was going. He, on the other hand, was floundering.

"I can see myself," she said when she looked down at her finished, polished pumps.

"Say, why didn't you get your polish on the way to Vegas? You're home now."

"You were busy when I came through here on departure," she said.

"But you don't need your shoes shined now," he said.

She smacked his shoulder with her open hand. "I'll make this easy for you." She dug into her hand bag she now had on her shoulder again and handed him her business card. "Give me a call sometime."

Benjamin stared at her card, silent. Her real name was Amy.

"You can still call me Persephone," she said. "Please do."

"Yes," he said.

"If I was psychic," she said as she stepped away.

"Are you?" he asked.

"No, silly. I'm making a prediction here. If I was psychic, and I'm not, I would say you won't call me. That will make us both sad."

He scrutinized her. It almost seemed like she was playing with him. About having visions. About seeing the future. The both of them.

"Prove me wrong, Benjamin," she said and walked away.

His mind whirled at their conversation. Did he introduce himself?

"Hey, Persephone, how did you know my name? I don't think I gave it."

She stopped and turned and considered him. She pointed at the sign above the raised platform with chairs where it read *Benjamin's*.

"Is it yours or your father's name?" she asked.

"Both. I'm junior."

"Just one date, junior," she said. "Maybe?" She raised her hand, palm up, in a don't know gesture. Then she turned around.

The ball was in his court. He had her number in his hand. He went over to the small trash bin next to the stand and he held the business card over the maw of it, his hands ready to tear the business card apart.

One thing that gave him pause was the pain of proving her *right*. That she was correct, he wouldn't call. He felt like he would be hurting her and he didn't like that.

But would it be any better if he died after they dated more than a year?

He groaned and his shoulders sagged. He rubbed his thumbs along the top edge of her card and found he didn't have enough strength to tear it.

When he stepped away from the trash bin he didn't have to be a psychic to know if he didn't tear up the card, he would call her.

And let fate unroll its course, as if he hadn't had a vision of his corpse at all.

THE LAST SURVIVING GONDOLA WIDOW

KRISTINE KATHRYN RUSCH

Kristine Kathryn Rusch is a New York Times *and* USA Today *bestselling writer and maybe the most award-winning and prolific writer working today. She has won more awards in science fiction and mystery than just about anyone and she is the only person to win the Hugo Award for her writing as well as her editing.*

She writes under three major names, Kristine Kathryn Rusch, Kris Nelscott, and Kristine Grayson. Plus a few minor names.

This story is set in an alternate time Chicago and is just amazing. You can find out a lot more about Kris's work at her publisher, WMG Publishing Inc www.wmgpublishinginc.com or her website www.kriswrites.com

THE LAST SURVIVING GONDOLA WIDOW

KRISTINE KATHRYN RUSCH

I slipped in for the motion picture. Regalese had set up a private screening in a tiny little theater near 19th and Dearborn, on the other side of the street from Bed Bug Row. I felt itchy just being there, and not only because of the proximity to the vice clubs, but also because I felt obviously out of my element.

Still, I dressed for the neighborhood. I wore my bobbed hair under an engineer's cap I confiscated from one of the Gondola widows when I found her years before. My baggy shirt and filthy overalls hid my assets, such as they were, but one of the other Pinkertons told me—kindly, he thought—that it was impossible to hide the female nature of my backside.

The memory of his comment always reminded me to wear everything baggy except my steel-toed boots. I would put a little bit of char on my face, and I'd learned to grunt low and hard whenever I wanted to say hello or goodbye or get the hell out of my way. I kept my head down a lot too.

Not that it mattered much in this theater. Designed for

burlesque shows mostly, the theater had a red velvet curtain that pulled back to reveal a real silver-painted screen. The screen was the fanciest thing about the place.

Regalese sat on benches with straw scattered across the floor beneath to absorb the crap on the patrons' foul-smelling boots. The straw hadn't been changed in weeks, if ever. Even though Regalese and I were the only two people in here, besides the projectionist and the organist, the place still stank of tobacco, sweat, and human fluids of a kind I didn't want to contemplate.

Regalese had told me to come for the motion picture, but hadn't told me how he'd first seen it. I wasn't sure I wanted to know, either. I worked with men who patronized the Levee District, but I liked to pretend they didn't.

The gaslights dimmed, and the motion picture started up. The organist started blaring some mock Sousa march, which besides being deafening was just damn offensive, given the nature of the images we were about to see.

Some so-called director had taken stereoscopes, still photographs, and silver addies, and had somehow—*Using His Own Magical Abilities!* the poster in the lobby blared— combined them into a herky-jerky semblance of a real film.

I didn't need to see the pictures, even speeded up. I'd been on Michigan Avenue the day the Gondolas died, and what was flickering on that screen was nothing like what really happened.

When I tell that story, I leave out most of the details. Like the way Chicago smelled before the attack. The city smelled new. The recently completed buildings were made of terracotta, marble, brick, and limestone. When the downtown air wasn't smelling like Lake Michigan fish, it smelled of newly milled stone dust. After the Great Fire, the city fathers had mandated all new construction—especially downtown—be made of fireproof stone.

I'd moved to the city five years after the fire, and had fallen in love immediately. The day the Gondolas died hadn't changed my love affair with the Windy City. In some ways, that day had reinforced it.

That day, I'd been on the job. I was the third woman Allan Pinkerton had ever hired in Chicago. The other two no longer worked for him. One had died—murdered horribly—and the other had fled when she realized what the job entailed.

Me, I found freedom in investigations. The role-playing, the games, that tiny bit of magic I could use to add a luster to everything, all combined to make me one of the city's greatest detectives. When no one could figure out what happened, the Pinkertons got called in. When no Pinkerton could figure out what happened, they called me.

Which was why I was just outside Cook County Bank & Trust that spring morning, dressed like a proper woman on a hot day. Shirtwaist, skirt with bustle, long auburn hair pinned to the top of my head, parasol to keep out the sun, and (for my sins) a corset, cinched so tight I hoped like hell I wouldn't have to run after anyone. The high-button shoes I wore with enough heel to help me pass for five-seven wouldn't have made it easy either.

I was supposed to determine bank balances by portraying the young wife of our target, an elderly millionaire who claimed he no longer had the funds to pay us. I'd been fighting to close the parasol before going inside, which was why I was on the sidewalk when someone gasped and pointed. Gondolas covered the sky over Lake Michigan like multicolored storm clouds. The whirring sound of their spikey engines sounded like heavy rain on water.

We'd heard about the Gondolas, but most of us hadn't believed they existed. Not in America anyway, and certainly not made by the South. Reconstruction had ended the year before, and everyone knew the South was bankrupt. How it could afford not one, not two, but several fleets of Gondolas stretched the imagination.

Only later, we learned that Great Britain supplied much of the material in exchange for cotton. Britain really didn't want the cotton as much as it wanted to see the Gondolas in action—

And it got to. The day the Gondolas died was the reason Britain stopped nurturing its own Gondola fleet and started building more ironclads instead.

But that switch was years away. We had to go through the horrors of that day, the death, the destruction, and what some call the Second Great Chicago Fire, before we came out the other side.

Or before some came out the other side.

The rest of us remained enmeshed in the War of Southern Aggression, even though the battlefield had emptied.

The motion picture captured none of that day's essence, although it had much of the day's symbolism. The Sousa march didn't help. All that happy brass music, with a parade beat, made me want to steal Regalese's pistol and shoot the organist in the back of his pomaded head.

Instead, I sat on my bench, hands clasped, watching moving images I'd seen before as photographs. The images didn't move naturally or even well, which was good, since I probably would have run screaming out of the theater if the motion picture had been anything close to accurate.

The motion picture was set up well. First, the Gondolas appeared, their artistic sphere-shaped balloons hovering over Chicago, perilously close to the great stone buildings on Michigan Avenue. Then the images became distant, showing the clouds gathering over Lake Michigan. The images clicked and clicked and it became clear that those clouds weren't clouds at all, but hundreds more Gondolas, coming in from the South, ready to rain hell on the Midwest's greatest city.

Then the sparks, like tiny fairy creatures, spread out across the sky, looking like flaws in the photographs, followed by the next series of images—fires erupting on all of the Gondolas, smoke pluming, the sky alternating dark and light.

Finally, the motion picture focused on the destruction: the Gondolas breaking apart, falling to the buildings below—shattering the Tiffany skylight of the Cook County Bank & Trust—and landing, in flaming pieces, on the streets and Grant Park and into the lake itself.

I shuddered. I couldn't help it. That day, the stupid parasol had saved me. If I had gone up the marble steps and through the brass handled double doors, I would have been one of those pathetic creatures burned alive inside Cook County Bank & Trust, after being showered with expensive glass and pelted with flaming Gondola parts.

No one had survived the inferno inside that bank.

No one.

When I had realized what was happening, I had run up the bank stairs. I had figured we had to pull people out before the situation got worse (I had no idea how bad it was) but as I reached the top of the steps, the windows exploded outward.

I ducked, covered my face, and screamed as shards penetrated the back of my hands and arms. My black skirt, shirtwaist, and corset protected me from damage anywhere else, although I did spend the evening trying to clear slivers from my waist-length auburn hair.

That was the night I bobbed my hair, not because I was making a political statement years before the rest of America's women would, but because I couldn't get all of the glass out.

That day was more than images. It was smoke so black and smelly that anything it touched had to be destroyed. It was the stench of burning canvas and searing flesh. It was heat so intense that skin dried and turned red blocks away from the flames.

It was—and I can attest to this—hell on earth.

The motion picture made the disaster look small. Tiny Gondolas, sparks like fireflies, smoke rising from the multicolored balloons—and the silence, always the silence, because the images made no noise.

Or maybe I couldn't hear anything. The organist was supposed to have been playing, but I didn't hear it. I got lost in the memories.

That day had been filled with noise, noise that still woke

me from a sound sleep. Screams and cries for help, sirens and the roar of flames, explosions and more explosions, followed by even more explosions.

My hands are still scarred from the burns I received as I grabbed a metal doorknob, as I tried to put out burning clothing before it seared flesh. My own magic, a little tiny bubble of protection, protected my skirts from catching fire. Still, like so many others, I ran to Lake Michigan. I plunged my arms into water—frigid despite the burning bits of debris on its surface—and that, doctors later said, prevented loss of motion.

I clenched my scarred hands as the images continued. Up —the burning sky; down—the fleeing and injured humans. Up —the debris falling off terra cotta roofs; down—the smoldering pieces of Gondola lying in the street.

The motion picture ended with a snap-snap-snap of the projector, and the bright silver light of an empty screen.

"See her?" Regalese asked.

I frowned at him. Regalese was fifteen years older than I was, a wanderer who had come to Chicago for the hunting after the day the Gondolas died. He freelanced for the Pinkertons. They didn't like his trigger-happy nature, even as they relied on it.

"Her?" I asked.

"Run it again," he said to the projectionist. I started to protest, but he grabbed my hand in his own. I knew he felt the crabbed, scratchy quality of my damaged skin, and I knew he didn't care.

The organist sat up, hands over the keyboard.

"Without music," Regalese added.

The motion picture started again. I wanted to close my eyes against the images, but I didn't. I made myself watch.

Regalese hadn't let go of my hand. I think he had expected me to look away, because he shook my fingers as one of the Gondolas toppled onto State Street.

"See her?" he asked again.

I squinted. The imagery had changed, away from the Gondolas and onto the poor unfortunate souls burning, and dying, their bodies littering the streets of this great city.

"See?" he asked, still shaking me.

The images were overlaid on each other. I had no idea how the compiler had done this, made it all look like it was actually moving, but when I stared I could see the different photographs, and this series had been taken in sequence.

Debris fell. People injured. Some looked up. Gondola basket toppled off the rooftop. People fled.

A woman fled.

She was thin and dressed in an oilskin coat with a matching cap, a bandana, and engineer's goggles around her neck.

A Gondola widow, big as day, escaping south.

A lot of Gondola widows escaped that day. Gondola *wives* as they still thought of themselves that afternoon. Widows only came later, when it became clear they would be considered heroes if they managed to get back to the South.

Warriors all of them, defending God and country—the Unrepentative Confederate States of America. Feted, celebrated, protected.

Until Reconstruction began anew in the aftermath of the attack, shoved down the throats of the unreformed Rebels by the dogged determination of the Congressional delegation of the Great State of Illinois.

"What's so special about her?" I asked.

"You don't recognize her?" He turned toward me.

I squinted, waved my hand, made the projectionist run the damn motion picture again. There she was, running, a half-turn toward the camera, a shot of fear. I was about to ask for the actual photograph when my brain supplied the answer Regalese was seeking.

"Oh, my god," I said. "That's Maizy Farmington."

First Lady. Wife of the current Governor of the Great State of Illinois.

————

It's bad form to accuse the wife of the Governor of treason against the Republic without some kind of proof. Especially in an election year. Proof wasn't hard to get against Gondola widows, but making proof stick, making it seem like it wasn't a dirty trick played by Governor Farmington's opponent—that was a little harder.

We needed witnesses other than ourselves. And that wasn't the usual way Regalese or I worked.

We'd caught dozens of Gondola widows in the aftermath of the day the Gondolas died. Gondolas, married to their female engineers, responded to the engineer's voice and the touch of her hand. First the voice. Then the Gondola would locate its engineer—its wife—and fly toward her.

What Regalese and I did was gather up the remaining pieces of the Gondolas and take them to potential widows.

The pieces would respond to the voice, and float to the engineer, identifying her as a Gondola wife/widow.

Once the women were identified by the remains of their Gondolas, most of the women broke into tears. They mourned the loss of their great flying warships as if mourning the loss of an actual spouse.

Many of the women believed their lives were no longer worth living, and gave up without a fight. The rest attacked us as if we personally had destroyed their ships.

We hadn't destroyed their ships. I couldn't have, and Regalese hadn't been here.

The real heroes of that day had been coalburners, most of whom had died for their bravery.

As the Gondolas gathered over the Mississippi, telegraph operators tracked them, growing alarmed at the increasing numbers of ships and the fact they had come from the Deep South. Messages about this impending crisis didn't come to the authorities; they traveled north through the coalburner network, tracking the ships.

Coalburners have a sparking magic, dangerous and hard to control. They use bits of the Earth—not just coal, but flint as well—to spark fires. Coalburners often have to live underground or on lakes, just to prevent fires.

And after the Great Chicago Fire, coalburners were banned from the city proper, although they snuck in to fight the Gondola attack. No one ever discovered who helped the coalburners onto the roofs of the city, and no one knew how they managed to coordinate the release of sparks, but everyone agrees that the coalburners saved us—even though all of the Chicago area coalburners had died that day.

I hadn't even noticed the coalburners, but I had seen some

of the newly created widows pull themselves from burning Gondolas. The women tried to flee, but most were too injured to get away.

Those that did get away hid in flophouses south of the Loop. It took little to track them down, and even less to identify them.

Regalese had joined our search in the weeks after the crisis, when it became clear that a handful of women had escaped the city. He and I partnered to find them—he often playing a jilted husband, and me a heartbroken sister as we enquired about lost loved ones.

We thought we'd caught all of them, until this motion picture showed up and revealed an even greater perfidy than we had realized. What was she planning for the Great State of Illinois?

"It shouldn't be hard to trap her," Regalese said to me as the moving images ended for a third time. "All we need are the Gondola pieces."

I bowed my head. He had moved to other jobs, including one investigating the magic behind moving images. That had been how he had discovered this bit of ephemera in the first place.

"Right?" he asked, his hand still holding mine.

I didn't want to speak in front of the projectionist or the organist. Instead, I thanked them both, stood, adjusted my overalls, and headed outside, blinking in the pale sunlight of the afternoon.

We stood alone on the sidewalk. The Levee didn't come alive until twilight.

"What am I missing, Lou?" he asked. He almost never used my name. No one in the Pinkertons did. It was too dangerous.

But he caught my mood, and he then needed my attention. My name was the only way to do so.

"We destroyed them," I said softly.

His eyes narrowed. He lived for the job, the hunt, the search for the next great magical threat. He stopped in Chicago only when he was in the area, when he needed the work, or when he had something to share with our version of the local constabulary.

"Destroyed what?" he asked, even though his tone told me he suspected what I was about tell him.

"Every last bit of the Gondolas," I said.

"Because...?" he asked.

"Because they started to reassemble, and we had no engineers that we trusted," I said.

He looked away. He knew I had just lied. We had an engineer, trustworthy and capable. She just wasn't willing. She had declined to bond with any kind of vessel, and she would continue to do so for the rest of her natural life.

I knew that for a fact—because that particular engineer was me.

———

Large magics, small magics, we all have a mix of them. My largest reservoir of magical talent fell into the engineering category. I could make machinery dance, and if I wanted to become part of it, let it chew a bit of my soul, I could make it do my bidding as long as it (and I) existed.

But I had embraced my small magic, the glamour that got people to talk to me, the tiny glow that made the casual observer look away unable to remember exactly what my voice sounded like, and what my face looked like. Perfect for detection. Less dramatic, and less emotionally exhausting than engineering magic.

At least, it had been until the day the Gondolas died. Then I had to go after women just like me, women who had made a different choice, women who had decided to give up their entire lives, their entire beings, to a ship and someone else's dream.

In the case of these Gondolas, the dream had been a second Civil War. It had failed so far, although many of us believed a third Civil War might flare up if the Federal Government ever did away with Second Reconstruction. I tried to ignore the punishing cruelty of that new system, which had started as retaliation for the near-loss of my city, by staring at my hands, and realizing that so many Chicagoans never came home the day the Gondolas died. All those people had done was go to work, visit a bank, or sit on a park bench, enjoying an afternoon by the lake.

"A new Gondola won't do, will it?" Regalese asked.

I shook my head. "She simply could refuse to ignite her magic."

I had done that countless times.

"We need her ship," I said.

Her ship from years before. Her ship from the attack. Her ship, which I knew, had already been destroyed.

———

I t took planning to approach her. I couldn't do it alone without revealing myself as engineering/magical. Regalese needed to be there to interrogate.

But we both knew that interrogations wouldn't work, at least in this instance. We would have to find another way to work.

I contacted the head of the detective agency, Allan Pinkerton, and asked him to use his contacts. Allan knew everyone who was anyone, and he'd lost a lot of personal friends on the day the Gondolas died. In fact, he'd lost so many friends that he hated the way the news rags had labeled the day, thinking the label should be closer to the day Chicago died. So many elites died in the firestorm because they'd been at their banks or their high-class offices or tending their high-class hotels.

They—or what was left of them—were all buried at Graceland Cemetery, so that Chicago's royalty could stride into the afterlife together.

I planned to use Chicago's royalty, which was something I didn't tell Allan. Because he was going to be appalled.

But my initial plan—using survivors of the attack—hadn't just been cruel; it had been heartless. Because there had been a good chance they could have died.

So once I formulated that plan, I tossed it without telling Regalese.

I came up with another plan. One I thought more benign.

Somehow, Allan convinced the head of the War Widows and Orphans Fund to hold a ceremony honoring the war dead. The Governor, a Union veteran, loved those kinds of events. He had a series of speeches that somehow roused the crowd, and made everyone decide to vote for him. He even made cemeteries feel like the appropriate place to hold a rally.

I'd seen him speak several times, but I'd never heard his wife talk. The newspapers claimed Illinois' First Lady was shy and retiring, standing beside her man, but never speaking for him—the way a proper woman should.

Such a vision of womanhood.

Such a lie.

I made sure that Allan insisted the only way the governor could talk was if Maizy laid a wreath on the monument to the Gondola dead. Maizy had to give a small speech before she set the wreath down. She couldn't have the governor do it for her.

For a few days, the governor's office tried to negotiate the conditions—apparently Maizy claimed she got ill whenever she had to address a crowd. But someone—Allan, the head of the fund, *someone* convinced Maizy (or, more likely, convinced the governor) that to lay a wreath without comment would be a slap in the face to the entire city.

I had chosen that location inside Graceland carefully. It was in the center of elite row, where so many of the wealthy dead from that day rested.

What I had forgotten until I approached the crowd that stormy afternoon was that the monument to the Gondola dead wasn't far from Lorado Taft's sculpture, *Eternal Silence*, which some wag had named "The Statue of Death." The creepy thing was as tall as a person, and was faceless, with an arm raised over the empty hood, blocking the place where a mouth would be.

I saw more than one attendee stop in surprise as they saw the statue. Even Regalese stopped, eyes wide as he looked at me.

"Wow," was all he said.

Wow, indeed.

The Gondola Dead monument paled in comparison. It had taken the city years to decide what to do. So many locals wanted a memorial downtown, but the businessmen and Governor Farmington (under the influence of his wife?) did not want reminders near the heart of the city. So the monument got shuffled to Graceland, and became smaller and less ornate as the designs went through various stages.

Now it was just a bronze spire, with a square base embossed with that day's date and some pious statement I had forgotten the wording of, and couldn't currently get close enough to see. Not that it mattered. What mattered was the wreath, the podium, and the fact that Maizy Farmington had arrived.

Appropriately, Maizy Farmington wore black. The outfit almost looked like widow's weeds, but was a bit too fashionable for that. The skirt was short enough to show her ankles (appropriately covered in well-worn high button shoes) and the blouse was covered with a gray shawl that seemed somber but didn't make Maizy Farmington look like she was mourning.

About a hundred people showed up on this fine morning. More than I would have expected, given the haphazard nature of the invitation to this event. Surprisingly, to me at least, a goodly number of the crowd were women even though we weren't allowed to vote. I suspected most of them had husbands or male family members they thought they could influence.

Influence. I didn't exactly know her agenda, but I knew that Maizy Farmington was like all the other wives out there. She did what she could to influence her husband.

Heaven knew what kind of subtle damage her whispers in his ear had done. The power behind the throne—and he probably hadn't even realized it.

I stood at the back of the crowd, behind two women with hats that had more feathers than half the birds in the state. I didn't want my magic to be obvious to Maizy, and I achieved that at this distance.

Regalese stood behind the people who had gathered closest to the podium. I warned him that he needed to stay away from Maizy. He was clearly trying to stay close but far away at the same time.

He knew what was coming.

Or what I hoped was coming.

I also hoped that Maizy didn't know. She had fled that day; she had no idea what people had died of. She probably thought everyone died of burns.

In fact, I had thought that too, until I focused some while thinking of that initial plan. Initially, I had thought to use survivors to reveal Maizy's treachery. Most of those survivors still had Gondola fragments stuck inside their bodies. The burning fragments had gone in, cauterized the wounds, and had somehow prevented gangrene or other horrid deaths.

But, I realized, many of the dead also had Gondola shrapnel in their bodies. Most of the dead had died of something else—flames, falls, too many wounds. Still, I was counting on that shrapnel to make my case.

And if Maizy Farmington actually knew how people had died, she never would have shown up.

But she was here, fidgeting beside her husband, clutching a mourning wreath in her black gloved hands. A phalanx of women from the War Widows and Orphans Fund stood behind her, as if being close to her conferred some validity upon them.

The governor stood beside her. He had pushed his hat back

from his face, and he kept looking sideways at her as if he expected her to bolt. Twice he leaned over and squeezed her arm.

Everyone said he loved her. And if I had learned anything in this job, love was a treacherous thing.

Finally, the ceremony started with the head of the fund—a stout woman whose gray hair suggested her status as a Civil War widow—giving an interminable speech about what we owed our honored dead.

As she spoke, my cheeks heated. I had just found another flaw in my plan. I wasn't honoring the dead—at least in the way that their widows and children would want to see. It wouldn't mean much to catch a Gondola widow, not with the horrors these women were about to endure.

I needed to abort the plan.

I moved away from the women in the back, starting to thread my way to the front of the crowd. The only way I could stop Maizy from speaking would be to make my presence known.

I was halfway to the front when the head of the fund finished her interminable talk. She turned, and loudly introduced the First Lady of Illinois.

For a moment, Maizy looked terrified. Then she nodded and headed toward the monument. Even though the organization had insisted she speak, she clearly wasn't going to.

Then a man yelled, "Speech!"

As others took up the cry, I realized that the first shout had come from Regalese. I hadn't had a chance to warn him about the flaw in our plan.

"Speech! Speech! Speech!"

She headed doggedly toward the monument, and her

husband trod after her. He caught her arm. She shook her head, and he smiled at her, a pleading little smile that told me more about their relationship than I wanted to know.

Then he led her back to the podium.

She glanced at him, looking trapped. The shouters grew quiet. She whispered something.

"Speak up!" Regalese shouted.

"Can't hear in the back!" one of the women shouted.

Maizy closed her eyes, then squared her shoulders. "Ten years ago," she said, "a group of Rebels tried to reignite the flames of our late war…"

Popping sounds echoed all over the graveyard, followed by banging and thudding. I saw bits of wood propel themselves from belowground. Other pieces—some larger than I wanted to think about—slammed out of nearby crypts, making gigantic holes in the stone.

People screamed, and several men dropped to the ground, hands over their heads. Veterans, still reliving the war.

Maizy looked horrified. She raised a hand, and all of the wood gathered around her.

"Go away!" she screamed, waving her hand. "Go away! You'll ruin everything!"

I stepped over the prone bodies of the men, saw the sobbing women around me, and noted how many graves had burst open.

Maizy pivoted so that she could run away, but the wood itself trapped her. It was trying to rebuild itself into her Gondola—and there were a lot of charred and goo-covered pieces, so that it could probably make a small replica of itself.

The governor's face had gone white. His hat had fallen to the ground, revealing his bald head. The wood shoved its way around him as if he hadn't existed, and had gathered around her.

"Maizy," he said, trying to get close to her. "Maizy, what is this?"

But the wood pushed him away. Besides, it was pretty clear what this was: he'd been sleeping with the enemy, and he had just realized it.

Still, he tried to get close, only to be pushed away.

I passed the governor, saw even more pieces of wood approaching from farther away in the cemetery, along with bits of the metal gears.

Maizy was shaking her head, and muttering, "No, no, go away," over and over again, as if she had forgotten how to control her Gondola.

"Take off your gloves," I snapped in the same tone my mentor had used as she trained me on magical equipment.

Maizy stopped muttering. Her gaze met mine, and her mouth fell open as she understood I had a similar magic.

"You can control your Gondola with your hands," I said. "You know that."

"You do it," she said softly, so only I could hear her. "You know how. For the Cause. We've got to try again. You know that. You need to help me."

"I don't need to help you, you traitor," I said.

My words carried over the panicked screams of the crowd. Everything grew quiet, and everyone was suddenly watching me.

I didn't want them to look at me. I wanted them to see her.

"I'm not a traitor," she said to me. "I'm loyal to my country."

"The Confederate States of America," I said.

She glanced around the wood, still trying to reassemble, but she probably couldn't see how many people were actually watching us. The wood had almost completely encircled her.

"Like you," she said.

"I'm no Rebel," I said.

"Maizy." The governor sounded heartbroken. "Maizy, what's going on?"

"Let me tell you, Mr. Governor," I said. "You married the Last Surviving Gondola Widow."

At that moment, screams echoed around me. Women streamed forward, grabbing at Maizy, clutching her, pulling at her. The governor took a step back, then nearly fell as Regalese yanked him out of the way.

The wood was trying to form a protective shield, but the shield wasn't being designed by Maizy so it had no real shape. Or maybe she really had forgotten how to use her magic effectively. She still wore her gloves.

Then the women of the Widows and Orphans Fund behind her tackled her and threw her to the ground.

The shrieks and cries and shouts of fury did not rival the sounds I heard on the day the Gondolas died, but they were hideous all the same.

Regalese covered the governor's face as they both turned away. More widows and veterans ran to the podium and piled on the woman they had only moments before honored.

The governor shook off Regalese and ran back to the mess, trying to pull people away. The wood remained gathered in a circle. Then it confusedly reassembled into the places that the pieces had probably held when they were part of the Gondola.

Regalese pulled me away from the melee.

"You don't want to see this," he said.

But, weirdly, I did. I didn't want to climb into the pile and take my revenge. I had taken my revenge by arresting the Gondola widows, and making cases against them that then led to the arrest of the traitors who had masterminded this attack all over the South.

Clearly they were planning a new attack, and Maizy had been in position to prevent a response to it. Or channel information to the attackers. Regalese and I would inform the Pinkertons, and they would inform the government. The United States Government.

Not that they'd miss this event. It was hideous.

The wood wobbled in place, and then the pieces toppled to the ground. I let out a small sound, and realized what that meant.

Maizy Farmington was dead.

My heart twisted for a moment. Was I responsible for that? I had orchestrated this event, after all.

Then I realized that all it would have taken was one mistake on her part, one softly spoken word, one laugh at a rally, and shrapnel from any survivors in the audience would have come toward her, just like it had here.

She had managed for four years to remain silent. But those first words, spoken almost like a confession, had condemned her.

Regalese almost put his arm around me, then thought the better of it. He nodded, I nodded, and we left the cemetery, walking past the Statue of Death, past the entrance, and onto North Clark.

To our south, the city rose. The tall stone buildings, castles near the lake, dominated the downtown skyline.

They had survived the day the Gondola died, a testament

to the vision of the post-Fire leaders. The city—the *state*— would survive this as well.

Just like the country had survived the attempt at a Second Civil War.

Just like it would survive a third.

I squared my shoulders and glanced over at Regalese. Somehow we had stopped something big. And only because we'd been doing our job.

We'd found the last of the Gondola widows.

And I hoped to God we would never see any more.

THE CASE OF THE SHORTED CIRCUIT

J. STEVEN YORK

J. Steven York is a master at writing some of the most twisted and thoughtful stories being published. But at times he writes just wonderful and only slightly twisted real-world stories. This might be a romance, might be a mainstream story, or even a mystery. No way of knowing, but it most certainly is a Pulphouse story.

Steve has been publishing novels and powerful short fiction for over thirty years now, and before that he worked writing in the gaming industry. Steve is also doing a really fun and off-the-wall internet comic, one of which he has allowed me to put in each issue on the back page.

THE CASE OF THE SHORTED CIRCUIT

J. STEVEN YORK

"What are you doing up on that ladder, Mr. Perry?" The voice came from under my feet, and I shifted my grip, passed the screwdriver from one hand to another, and looked down into the accusative stare of Kevin, Julia's middle son. Appropriately for a middle son, he was in his middle thirties, slim and athletic, with a surfer's sun-bleached hair. He frowned.

"I'm just about to wire up the mounting plate for the flood-light. I turned off the breaker in your mother's office, and she's guarding it while I attach the wires."

"I really don't think you should be doing that," he said. "You wandered in and asked if you could help, I figured you meant taping some windows or something."

"Look, I learned some things about wiring when I was in the Navy."

"I'm guessing that was a long time ago. And anyway, that's not really the issue, It's the ladder."

I looked down at my feet and felt a few butterflies in my

stomach. The light was over the front door of the outbuilding, and I was pretty high. Heights were never my thing. I could climb a ladder if I need to, but after the three or four steps I start to get nervous. Still… "Look, I'm retired, not dead."

"Just the same, why don't you let one of us younger guys handle it later?"

I looked at the open electrical box and the three projecting wires. The ends were safely capped off with wire nuts so that wouldn't be a hazard if I stopped mid-job. I had my pride, but I didn't like ladders, and I didn't want to cause problems with Julia's three adult sons who had showed up to help repaint and spruce up her long-neglected house and shop/office building. "If you feel strongly about it," I said, and carefully worked my way back down the ladder to the concrete slab.

Jason, the dark haired older son appeared around the corner carrying a freshly cleaned extension roller, and looked at me curiously. From the other direction, youngest son, Leo appeared dressed in spattered painter's coveralls, goggles on his forehead pushing back a cresting wave of mousey brown hair that poked up above them like a hedge row.

I'd met all of them a few times when they were still living at home. But that had been years ago. The adult versions were virtual strangers to me, other than what Julia had told me about them.

Short version: Leo was the angry young artist, still finding his way. Kevin was the free-spirit outdoorsman, surfing, rock-climbing, hiking, and working just enough to finance his passions. Jason was the hands-on guy, dropping out of college to become a landscaper. None of them had turned out the way, Julia and her late husband had wanted. "Disappointed," was not quite the word. Something more along the lines of "sad" and "concerned."

I knew all of them struggled financially, and I had to suspect that had something to do with why they were all here now, three years after the death of their father. The peeling paint and delayed repairs on their mother's 1940's cottage were hardly a new development.

I looked at Kevin and pointed at the electrical box with the screwdriver. "If you aren't going to do it now, I'm going to turn the breaker back on. It's on the same circuit with your mom's office lights and plugs, and she's sitting there impatiently waiting to get back to work."

He grunted and I wandered inside the little outbuilding that housed her husband's old workshop and, in the back, her small writing office. I placed the screwdriver on the pegboard by the door so it could be found later, and glanced around the gloomy shop area, illuminated only by sun streaming in through a small window and the door.

Most of it was empty, the power tools sold off to make ends meet. Irwin's illness hadn't left much behind other than medical bills and debt. It had taken Julia years to wrestle it under control and she had barely held onto the house.

I knew more about her affairs than the bored and nosy retired lawyer from down the block should, because at one point, besides being casually social with them, I had been Irwin and Julia's attorney on several matters, and had been consulted more recently, only in a friendly capacity, when Julia wanted to write her own will and get her affairs in order. She assured me she was in fine health, but she didn't want to leave her sons with the kind of disorganized mess she'd had to deal with. I had encouraged her, but for actual legal work, I directed her to my daughter, Gail, who had taken over my practice when I decided to retire.

Without false modesty, I can say Gail is a very bright and promising young lawyer with a strong interest in family law, a direction she's been steering the practice since she took over.

Hell yes, I'm proud of her.

I rapped on the frame of Julia's open office door.

"Come in," she said. The room was small and blindingly pink with white trim, possibly personal preference, possibly the result of a modestly successful dalliance with writing romance novels that Julia had taken up until her husband's death. She'd published several, though she had confided that her biggest advance had been only a little over ten thousand dollars. Not much of a living, and far from making a person rich.

I blinked against the pink, broken by the gray breaker box panel in the wall directly across from the door, and a brown bookshelf next to it filled with what looked for all the world like a matched set of law books. I that they were actually a bound edition of the complete works of Earl Stanley Gardner, the creator of TV lawyer Perry Mason, who (previously unknown to me) had originated in a long-running series of novels. Julia said they were her favorites as a child. That's how she came to make the jump from romance to mystery-writing.

"Hi, M. Did you get that light hooked up?" Julia sat in an office chair in front of her darkened computer, her back swiveled to the window so she could read the manuscript pages in her hand.

"No. Kevin found me up on a ladder and shooed me away. I guess he didn't want to have to clean up my dry shattered bones when I fell to my death. He says one of them will take care of it later."

She laughed. "Kevin's always been the bossy one. His younger brother has always ignored him, and his older brother—well—he was older, and that settled that." But she seemed to drift back into her own thoughts for a moment, perhaps the result of contrasting her sons.

I flipped the breaker, and the overhead fluorescent—no, LED, I corrected myself -- fixture flickered on above us. I glanced around to make sure none of the three boys were in earshot. "Let me guess. You haven't figured out which one you're going to ask to be executor of the will?"

She frowned and shook her head. "Look, if you can spare a few minutes, I need to run to the post office and grab a sandwich before I get back to working on the second Nancy Lawborne mystery. I've got a deadline, and I'm letting myself get way too distracted by this. I could use a sounding board."

I grinned. "I have nothing but time."

She grabbed an addressed manila envelope and we jumped into the front of her battered blue minivan. The suspension squeaked at every bump, and the radio was broken, but the seats were okay and the air conditioning worked a little, so it was fine. "I really would have liked to have gotten an electrician for the lights and stuff, but after buying all the paint and supplies and renting the sprayer, I just didn't have the cash. Book money is coming—lots of it, but it's not here yet, and I still have to budget."

"The boys know this?"

"They do. Not the specifics, but none of them have ever seen much money, and I worry the idea will make them a little crazy."

"But you can handle it?"

"Irwin handled the finances and budgeting, at his insistence, but I was always the practical one. I humored him and kept my hands off, much to my regret. I worry the boys take after him."

"But you still need an executor."

"I want everything to be clear and in order. All cards on the table. I have to find the best of three very suspect candidates. I love my sons, but I'm not sure I understand any of them." She considered, then brightened. "Could Gail be the executor?"

I hesitated. "She *could*. You could ask her, anyway. But for an attorney to be the executor of a will they themselves drew up is getting into an ethically murky area, and my daughter tends to be conservative in such matters. The kid's as ethically scrupulous as a saint."

"Maybe that's a dumb idea anyway. The executor is going to have to handle my literary estate, and that's a very personal thing. I'd really like to keep it in the family."

"Seems reasonable," I said. I took a mental note to suggest that Gail brush up on intellectual property law.

"Look," I said, "I don't really know them at all at this point. I certainly can't help you decide. I'm just concerned that —well—I've seen the pursuit of money divide a lot of families. And if that movie option you mentioned goes anywhere... The word 'Hollywood' just makes a lot of people go crazy."

She smiled. "It makes me a little crazy too. I appreciate your referring me to an entertainment lawyer to handle the negotiations. I'm not equipped to swim with sharks like that."

"Neither am I," I said, silently adding, *any more*. I'd lost interest in business law when my wife died from a heart attack six years earlier, and I'd let Gail take the reins just as quickly as I could. But I was no happier with nothing to do but hang around the house and turn into the nosy and overly-talky neighbor that I had become. I was bored and adrift.

Without Mary, I had lost my anchor. I didn't know who I was, or what I was doing.

In trying to help with Julia's house, perhaps I was groping for that purpose. I could be a man and do something useful and productive again, or so I thought. But Kevin's rejection had just made me feel old and useless again. And secretly, I wondered if he'd been right. I'd been assigned temporarily to assist an electrician's mate for a few months in the Navy. I didn't have any of the specialized training, but they were at sea and short-handed when we're had to medivac a sailor with a burst appendix

Mostly I passed tools, held a flashlight, toted gear from deck to deck, and did really simple repairs under careful supervision. I knew a *little* about the wiring on a ship, at least the antiquated frigate I'd been serving on at the time, but that was a lot different that a modern house.

I remembered when Mary and I had redone our bathroom, and the electrician had to explain to me the legally required ground-fault detector, a special plug with a gizmo that instantly killed the power at the slightest hint of a short circuit. They had to have them in all potentially wet environments now. Maybe the ship had had them too, and I just didn't know about it.

I sat in the car while Julia ran into the post office, and despite my protests, she bought Italian subs for both of as at a great little family place down on Central Street. We ate at an outside table and pleasantly drifted into talking music, mystery movies, and the "good old days."

We arrived back at Julia's house to find the three sons standing around the ladder, animatedly arguing with each other. I noticed that the floodlight fixture had been installed while we were gone, and quickly realized that was the crux of the argument.

Jason stepped out ahead of the others. "Leo blew the circuit breaker somehow!"

"I did not," said Leo. "I just plugged the light in, and it went pop and the lights inside went out."

Kevin shrugged. "Well, you were the one fiddling with it when it went."

"Well," said Jason, ""It wasn't me! I was going to install the light, but I was in the shop reading the installation instructions. By the time I came out, Leo was up there plugging the light into that mounting plate gizmo.

I looked inside through the door to verify that Gail's office was dark again. "You tried resetting the breaker? Did it blow again?" I considered how the simply three-wire job of connecting the fixture *could* have created a short circuit.

"I turned it back on," said Kevin. "It didn't pop. Just nothing happened."

I considered what could be wrong. "You checked the master breaker?"

Leo looked confused.

Kevin frowned.

"Never mind," I said, heading for the breaker box.

I verified that the breaker for the office and lighting downstairs lights was on. I jiggled the lever and it seemed solid. I turned it off and back on again. No lights. I verified that the main breaker was on. I checked the lights in the storage loft upstairs and the plugs in the shop. They all worked fine.

They were on separate breakers.

I was mystified. The problem was on that one breaker, and that one circuit.

I walked back to the electric box and found the first outlet under the window and a few feet to the right of the Perry Mason bookcase. I imagined the wiring hidden in the walls, starting with that first plug, running through the outlets in a daisy chain, one by one around the office, then up into the ceiling through all the lights in the next room, and logically ending at that outside light.

Ending.

As far as I knew, nothing had changed in that circuit but the outside light. Nothing new had been plugged in here in the office. And there were no plugs outside the office, just ceiling lights that certainly hadn't changed. I remembered in the Navy, when the electrician's mate I reported to had told me to know my own limitations. "Know when something is above your pay grade, and don't hesitate to hand it off to an expert."

I reluctantly admitted that this was one of those times.

When I came back out, the argument had drifted over towards the back door of the house, but it was still going strong. In fact things had turned even more acrimonious, and Julia had stepped into the fray. There were accusations and criticisms flying in all directions, and they had everything, and nothing, to do with a dead electrical circuit.

Julia saw me walk up and turned hopefully. "Did you find anything?"

I shook my head sadly. "I think you really need to call in an electrician on this. I've eliminated all the obvious things I can think of. It has to be something weird and esoteric. Maybe a defective breaker, or a wire break somewhere inside the wall." I glanced over at the sons, "Unless one of you experts has any ideas."

They all just looked uneasy, shuffling their feet.

"I thought so." I focused my attention on Kevin. "You should have let me finish. I knew what I was doing. Having multiple people working separately on one project leads to mistakes and makes troubleshooting harder."

More lessons from that long-ago electrician's mate.

"Kevin didn't duck my stare. "You're right. But you looked a little shaky on that ladder. I didn't want you hurt."

He seemed sincere.

The boys had calmed, but Julia just seemed more agitated. "It's after five on a Friday. Even if I can get an electrician on the phone, no telling when they can come out, and it's going to cost three times as much, if not more! I don't have the money just laying around, and neither do any of you three clowns! All over money that I don't even have yet, and that none of you will hopefully see for a *long* time!"

They just stared at her, mouths open.

"I have a deadline, a book to finish. I've fallen behind because of this project and all your arguing. And my office is blacked out, probably for the whole weekend, if not longer. No books, no money for *anybody!* All because you're squabbling over my favor. Well let me tell you, *none* of you are looking good right now!

"I thought maybe I could pick one of you to act as the executor of my will, but I see now that what I really need is a *keeper* for the three of you!" She headed for the back door of the house. "I'm going to go put a call in to my editor and warn her I may miss my deadline."

Everybody was looking as crushed as I'd felt a few a few minutes earlier. I found some previously missing empathy with them. "I'm sorry. I had hoped maybe I could puzzle this out and defuse the situation."

Leo gave me a look of contempt. "Fat lot of good you did!"

"He's right," said Jason, looming closer. "We've seen you hanging around her. How do we know you aren't the one after her money?"

"I'm a retired attorney," I said. "I'm not rich, but I've got my own money, thanks. And I remind you that she doesn't yet have any money. She's spent most of what she's gotten catching up bills and paying for these house repairs.

"I'm trying to help because I've known your family for a long time, and I've see what hard times you've *all* gone through. I'd happily lend your mom whatever she needs to get through, but I know she's too proud to even consider the offer. So I thought I could at least lend a little elbow grease.

"I'm sorry you three don't see it that way. Well, you're on your own now. I'm going home. If your mom wants me, she can call."

I was half-way down the block, counting the cracks in the sidewalk, feeling angry and dissatisfied on every level, when I heard the steps of someone running up behind me. I glanced back and saw Kevin, already braking to drop in beside me and match my rapid walk.

"Listen Mr. Perry. I owe you an apology. I wasn't entirely truthful back there."

I slowed my pace to a stroll. "I'm listening."

"First of all, it was true, I *was* worried about you on the ladder. But I also wanted to get the light fixed and get mom's office power back on to make myself look good. I was trying to be the hero." He hung his head. "I know this is all stupid, the way my brothers and I are fighting. But that's just how we are."

I nodded. "I have a brother too."

"It's not about the money, or being executor really, not for me anyway. It's just something to jockey over, a way of keeping score."

"You're adults. Maybe it's time to start acting like it."

He nodded. "You're right. Absolutely. I'm always the guy trying to take charge. Nobody listens to me. Leo just doesn't, and Jason just won't. But this time I'm starting to see I don't deserve to be in charge. I don't know anything about estates, or books, or any of this stuff. I couldn't even follow a simple set of-- I don't know how, but..."

I continued his sentence. "But you're the one that wired that mounting plate into the electrical box."

"How did you know?"

I smiled. "Elimination. Leo knew so little about what he was doing he'd never have figured out the mounting plate and got the wires hooked up. Jason was still reading the instructions when the problems started. You were the first to know the problem, and so had a head start. You were rushing to get the office power back on."

He nodded. "I glanced at the instructions. It looked simple enough and so I threw them back in the box, grabbed a screwdriver, and went right to it."

"But then you got called away somehow."

"I finished putting in the plate, and ran into the house for a quick pee break. Mom stopped me on the way back to chew me out about chasing you off the ladder. And when I finally got back, Leo was up already up there finishing the job. I was about to yell at him when the lights went out."

"And you knew it was your fault."

"Because the light itself just has a little three pin plug on the bottom that plugs into that terminal block on the base where the wires hook up. It's idiot proof. Even Leo couldn't screw it up."

I looked him in the eye. He didn't flinch."But you were willing to let him take the fall for it."

"It was childish, but I figured he had it coming for trying to take the credit. But I was wrong. I should have owned up."

"Yes," I said, stopping in the sidewalk and turning back. "You should have. But you owned up to it eventually, and you recognized where you went wrong."

I blinked. "And I think I just recognized where I went wrong too!" I started walking back towards Julia's house. I turned back and waved Kevin to follow me. "Come on. I could use somebody to pass the tools and hold the ladder. Let's see if we can fix this thing.

"Tell me Kevin, how do you interrupt a circuit from the end of the line?"

He shrugged. "I don't know."

"From the beginning," I said.

Our first step was to eliminate the short circuit I knew had to be there. The short circuit that wasn't the problem, just the trigger.

I climbed up the ladder (Kevin braced it from the bottom) and removed the two screws that held the light onto the bracket, exposing the terminal block that Kevin has mentioned, and that I knew about from my own reading of the instructions.

The mistake was immediately clear. The plastic terminal block was supposed to hold the three wires in holes in the *side*, which were clamped down with screws. The light itself had a three pin plug that connected to the three holes in the *top* of the block. Only Kevin had misunderstood and inserted the wires into the *top* of the terminal block, keeping the pins from plugging in properly. With no place to go, the pins had bent, hitting the screws and bridging the ground wire with one of the other two, and creating a short circuit.

I carefully removed the wires and capped them off with wire nuts.

Then we went to Julia's empty office. I looked at the bookcase. The set of books didn't completely fill the shelf. There were a few gaps filled with various knickknacks. "Gardner, you sly old fox, you still have a few mysteries to keep."

Julia appeared in the door behind us. She looked considerably calmer than the last time I'd seen her.

"What's going on?" she asked. "I had a talk with my editor. I could tell she wasn't thrilled, but she said I could have those extra days if I need them. A week even if I *really* need it."

"That's great," I said, "but maybe you won't need them." I bent down to the second shelf from the bottom, removed a decorative glass pot, and peered into the dim space behind. I could just make out a previously hidden plug, and on it a little glowing LED light. I reached for it, found the reset button, and pushed.

The ceiling lights instantly flickered on.

Julia gasped. "How?"

I pointed to the plug behind the shelf. "This plug, hidden and presumably forgotten behind the shelf, is a ground-fault plug. It's designed to detect even the smallest short on the circuit and shut it down before someone can be electrocuted or a fire can start. They're used on any circuit in a potentially wet location. An outside light fixture would count I imagine, maybe a workshop as well. I'd have to read the zoning statutes. And once the ground fault plug is tripped, it interrupts the circuit until manually reset with this little button."

"We don't need an electrician?"

"I'll still need to hook up the floodlight, but I know how to do it." I looked at Kevin, who was grinning at the revised state of the world. "Or Kevin could do it, once we take a good look at the instructions and clear a few things up."

"I'll go find the box the light came in," said Kevin slipping past us and out the door.

"Take your time. I want to talk to your mom for a few minutes." I closed the office door behind him.

She smiled, shaking her head. "Thank you!"

I shrugged. "I was giving up and heading home when Kevin caught up with me. He helped me to put it together. Turns out I do at least know a *few* things about wiring!"

"And solving mysteries."

"Maybe."

I hesitated, wondering where exactly I should stick my noisy neighbor nose. But maybe in this case, I was acting more as friend of the family. "Look, you seemed pretty fed up with your sons and the whole executor thing."

"I was angry—and afraid. I've never missed a deadline before, and this book contract is important to me, in more ways than one."

"I can't tell you what to do, but when you're calm enough to think about it, you might take another look at Kevin."

She looked skeptical. "I'm just saying I see some potential

in him. A mystery is about who-done-it. But in adulthood, it's sometimes more important who *didn't* do it."

She shook her head, confused.

"Never mind. Just give him a thought. Make up your own mind."

"Sure." But then her mind seemed to go somewhere else, and she slowly smiled.

"This all give me some ideas for book three! But I'll have to change things around a bit."

"I suppose there will have to be a murder."

"Is it a mystery if there isn't a murder?"

"You're the expert."

"Speaking of book three, when I turn this thing in, I want to get an immediate start. I've got some legal questions a retired attorney might be able to help me with."

"Sure," I said. And then the words tumbled out, unexpected. "Let me buy you dinner."

Both of us looked surprised. But I rolled the idea around in my mind. I missed Mary every day, but she was gone, and this seemed less like a betrayal than an inevitable evolution.

I was moving again.

Where I didn't know.

I wondered if Gail could use an investigator...

A CRAFTY CHRISTMAS

ANNIE REED

Professional writer Annie Reed writes stories that span genres and are always powerful. In fact with Annie, you just never know the type of story you might be reading, but you will always know it will grab you and be a compelling read.

With this story, Annie gives us a nifty Lifetime Holiday Movie set-up, but then makes the story into a pure Annie Reed story you will love. So far Annie has had a story in every issue of Pulphouse and as the editor, I hope to continue that streak.

Her story "The Color of Guilt" was selected for The Year's Best Crime and Mystery Stories. *Look for so much more of this prolific writer's work at her website https://anniereed.wordpress.com/*

A CRAFTY CHRISTMAS

ANNIE REED

The last person on earth Kelsey Nichols expected to run into at her aunt's favorite stitchery store the Saturday after Thanksgiving was her old high-school boyfriend. Rory Demeter had been the first (and only, if she was being honest with herself) person she'd ever loved, and the first (and last, she'd sworn to herself) person to ever break her heart.

Pain like that once in a lifetime was enough, especially since she'd still loved him like crazy when they broke up, and she was pretty sure he still loved her. But when you're sixteen years old and your seventeen-year-old boyfriend's family moves out of town for his dad's new job—*way* out of town, like northern Nevada to Hawaii out of town—a month of emails and phone calls was enough to convince the both of you that a long-distance relationship just wasn't going to work.

Then there'd been the different kind of pain—the deep ache of grief—when her parents died in an automobile crash four years later while Kelsey was away at college. Never, ever again would she allow herself to really love someone, not even a pet. The cost was too great. So she'd thrown herself into her schoolwork, earning a bachelor's degree in communication (with honors, thank you very much) and a minor in digital media, and kept working just as hard toward her masters.

As her best friend Tisha joked, Kelsey was all set to become the smartest damn blogger on the planet.

What Kelsey really wanted to do after college was help small businesses connect better with their customers through the use of digital media. Digital media was the way businesses of the future would do business, much easier and less messy (not to mention cheaper) than having to deal with people in person. The online retail giants had certainly proved that, but small businesses could learn how to compete in their own way, she was sure of it, and they didn't have to outgrow their ability to serve their customers to do it. She couldn't wait to get out in the real world and show people that digital media didn't have to be simply click-bait headlines and in-your-face webpages that all ended up looking pretty much the same.

But this last semester had been hell. Between her work as a graduate assistant and her own studies, she'd been so burned out she not only questioned her career choice, she questioned whether she even had one single original (or semi-original) idea to offer anyone.

She'd really been looking forward to her usual holiday plans: Thanksgiving dinner with Tisha splurging on sushi at their favorite Asian fusion restaurant, followed by two weeks of recouping her energy and catching up on her studies in her blessedly quiet room since most of the undergrads in her dorm went home for the holidays or in an isolated study carrel in the campus's mostly deserted library. She was even looking forward to catching a bus for the two-hour trip to her Aunt Adeline's little house tucked into the forested foothills south of Reno to spend the rest of her holiday break, including Christmas day, with her only living relative. She could put in her earbuds, play her favorite holiday music, and get lost in actually reading a book for pleasure—one of the best parts of winter break.

This year all those plans went up in smoke. Literally.

One of the undergrads had fallen asleep with a candle in their room the night after finals. The resulting fire had been doused quickly and efficiently by what Tisha described as the hottest men she'd ever seen. Kelsey agreed that there certainly appeared to be a reason firefighters starred in all those beefcake calendars year after year if the firefighters who'd reported to the dorm were any indication. (She might be relationship avoidant, but she wasn't dead. She didn't have any problems appreciating the male form—from afar.)

Unfortunately, thanks to the fire, the school had to close down the entire dorm for repairs and to give the city time to re-inspect the building before letting residents back inside. The school estimated three weeks before the dorm would open up again. It was, after all, the holidays, the email from the administrative office pointed out, rather apologetically.

Tisha roomed in the dorm down the hall from Kelsey, which meant the fire left them both homeless for the holidays. Tisha's parents invited their daughter to move back home temporarily, and made it clear Kelsey could come along too. The guest room in their Napa Valley house was big enough for two, but Kelsey had never been to Napa, much less met Tisha's parents. She didn't want to spend her holiday break with strangers, not after the semester she'd just had. But she certainly couldn't afford to rent a hotel room for days on end.

Aunt Addy, with her usual unflappableness, had suggested that Kelsey simply spend her entire winter break with Addy at her little A-frame house in the woods.

"You can come here and have Thanksgiving dinner with me this year," she'd said. "I won't be serving sushi"—Addy knew about Kelsey's non-traditional Thanksgiving dinner, but Addy hated any kind of fish; the thought of eating raw fish horrified her—"so you'll have to do traditional. I tend to over-cook for the holiday anyway, and it'll be nice to have someone around to help me eat all the leftovers."

Overcook was an understatement. Aunt Addy had always been the best cook in the family, and she always made too much food. Admittedly, now that their family numbered exactly two—Addy and Kelsey—and since Kelsey couldn't cook more than instant ramen with any reliability, the bar wasn't exactly high.

Kelsey hadn't exactly jumped at the invitation. Spending an entire month with her aunt would either drive her the kind of crazy that only two independent women used to living alone could do to each other, or she'd get used to having family around and become too attached. Visiting with her aunt at Christmas had always worked out well in the past. Just about the time they were getting on each other's nerves, it was time to say goodbye for another year. And Kelsey never felt more than a momentary pang of sadness when she hugged her aunt for the last time before getting on the bus for the two-hour trip back to college.

One week was the perfect amount of time to keep her

emotional distance, even at such an emotional time as Christmas. An entire month?

That was going to take some work. She'd just have to be sure to keep some distance between the two of them.

So she'd said yes, which had thrilled her aunt if the enthusiastic "awesome!" from the other end of the call was any indication. That made Kelsey feel like the worst sort of Grinch for even thinking of saying no.

Addy actually cooked a relatively light Thanksgiving dinner for the two of them by Addy's usual standards—sliced turkey she must have purchased from a deli along with homemade stuffing and cranberry sauce, a delicious green bean casserole that put the old canned-soup variety to shame, and two pies, pumpkin and apple, complete with freshly whipped whip cream, for dessert. They laughed and talked about current events and Kelsey's classes and the critters that Addy saw when she went on hikes through the towering pines around her house.

"Mostly squirrels," Addy said, "but occasionally a deer or two," which Addy said had the softest brown eyes. "You could come with me, if you want."

Kelsey said she'd think about it, although she secretly hoped for snow. The dry pine needles that seemed to cover the ground everywhere made her sneeze, which was one drawback with spending so much time at Addy's house. But when it snowed? The little A-frame house looked like something out of a fairytale then, all brown-stained wood the color of gingerbread with soft tufts of snow on the sharply slanted roof and warm, golden light shining through the curtained windows, tucked in among towering pines frosted with snow.

When Kelsey had still lived in Reno with her parents, they

had a normal-looking house in a normal-looking subdivision, complete with mostly green lawns and trees that lost their leaves in the winter. Even when it snowed, the neighborhood didn't look all that special. But what she remembered the most, when she let herself think of her childhood, was the fun she had making snowmen in the backyard with her dad in the winter.

Sometimes the snowmen were dinky and crusted with dried leaves and dirt because it hadn't really snowed enough to cover the ground. But other times, when the snowfall was deep enough that her dad stayed home from work and the neighbor kids pulled a sled down the street, then her dad would help her make a proper snowman, complete with one of his knit hats and one of her mom's knit scarves.

Of course, memories like that inevitably led to memories of Rory.

The winter before his family moved to Hawaii, it had snowed almost every day in January. The snow had been soft and fluffy, like it was at Addy's house, and they'd spent far too much time having mock snowball fights that usually ended up with both of them rubbing glovefuls of snow in each other's face and hair. He'd had the darkest, thickest hair, and the deepest blue eyes that she'd spent hours gazing into. Those eyes had always seemed to sparkle with mischievous good humor whenever he looked at her.

She wondered what he was doing now. If he was having dinner with his family in Hawaii, and what kind of a Thanksgiving dinner that might be. A traditional turkey dinner, or maybe a pig roasted over a pit on the beach, or something even more exotic? Maybe he had sushi for dinner, too.

She sighed and gave herself a mental shake. It had been

months since she'd thought about Rory, and she wasn't doing herself any favors thinking of him now just because she'd be spending more time in the city where they both used to live.

After dinner, Addy asked whether Kelsey wanted to check out the Black Friday sales the next day. When Kelsey said she'd rather spend time reading, Addy let the subject drop.

Maybe this arrangement would work out well, after all.

Kelsey kept thinking that until Saturday morning when Addy suggested Kelsey go with her to a little craft shop.

"I'm just going to swing by for a few minutes," Addy said over toast and half a grapefruit. "I need to pick up a some more yarn for my pillowtop." She'd been stitching the day before on something that looked like a geometric optical illusion in various shades of red and green. "It'll be fun. Then you can get back to your reading."

Addy liked needlework crafts the same way Kelsey liked to read—almost as much as breathing. For as long as Kelsey could remember, Addy was always working on one project or another. It kept her hands busy, she used to say, while she watched (listened to, really) television or read (listened to, again) an audiobook.

The little room Addy jokingly referred to as her guest bedroom was really where she kept all her craft supplies and had her sewing machine set up. Kelsey didn't know where Addy must have moved all the folded pieces of fabric and boxes of yarn and plastic tubs of knitting needles and crochet hooks that usually took up space on and around the futon where Kelsey slept whenever she visited. In the past, Addy had simply stacked her supplies on the room's hardwood floor and on top of her sewing table.

This time, the room was remarkably free of crafty things.

Addy had even stored the sewing machine, and she'd transformed the sewing table into a bedside table of sorts, complete with a little windup alarm clock, a box of tissues, and a framed print of a selfie Kelsey had taken with her aunt on Christmas day the year before.

The print had touched her heart when she'd first seen it even more than her aunt's generous offer to extend her visit for an entire month.

Kelsey reminded herself that this visit was disrupting her aunt's life, too. Addy had obviously shoved her favorite craft supplies somewhere to get them out of the way. Would a trip to a crafts store really be that much of a hardship?

She blew on her steaming mug of hot chocolate to buy herself time to respond. She would rather have had a cup of coffee, or better yet, a skinny mocha latte. The coffee shop in the student union made a great skinny mocha latte, but she only allowed herself one per week. Two if her week was going to hell. Unfortunately, Addy wasn't born with the coffee gene; she was a chocoholic.

And right now she had a strange expression on her face, the kind of expression undergrads got when they really wanted something really important from the professor and thought the professor's graduate student might put in a good word for them. Kelsey didn't have a crafty bone in her body and Addy knew it. So why did she want Kelsey to go to a craft store, of all things?

"I'll even buy you a coffee," Addy said. "One of my friends keeps telling me I should try this little kiosk on the other side of the parking lot from the crafts store. It's supposed to be great, and I know you like your lattes."

Okay, now something was truly up. Her coffee-avoidant

aunt was offering to buy her a designer drink from one of those drive-thru coffee places.

Addy wasn't trying to set her up, was she? She'd never done that before, and besides Addy had been single her entire life, too. She was the last person Kelsey expected would try something like that.

One thing she did know about her aunt was that the woman was persistent if she had her mind set on something. So Kelsey shrugged, willing to go along.

For now.

"But I'm holding you to the coffee deal," she said. "I bet they make hot chocolate, too."

Addy sipped at her own mug of hot chocolate, complete with remnants of melted mini marshmallows. "Twice in one day, how decadent," she said with a grin.

An hour later Kelsey wondered if she'd misread the entire situation. Maybe Addy just wanted the company. The tiny, overstuffed aisles at Stella's Stitchers were crowded with holiday shoppers, but so far, her aunt hadn't tried to introduce Kelsey to anyone, not even the spry sixty-something woman behind the register who'd said hello to Addy by name when they'd first come in the store.

While her aunt browsed through racks filled to over-flowing with small packages of yarn, reading numbers on the labels and comparing them to her handwritten list, Kelsey just tried to stay out of everyone's way. In some ways, the store reminded her of her favorite independent bookstore near campus—shelves crammed full with any kind of book a vora-cious reader might want. If she was into needle crafts, this store would be heaven. It certainly seemed that way to the women—and the occasional man—browsing through the racks and racks of colorful supplies.

Her cell phone buzzed in the pocket of her jacket. She retrieved it to read a text from Tisha accompanied by a selfie with her tongue sticking out and her eyes crossed. *Mom took me shopping,* the text read. *Augh!*

Kelsey chuckled. They were such mature grad students —not!

She was about to text back when she ran into an absolute wall of a man who had his back to her. Nearly a foot taller than Kelsey's respectable five-foot-six, solid muscle, broad shoulders, dark hair. Dressed in forest green tights, a red and green tunic, and a pointy green Santa hat, but somehow, even with his back to her, he made that outfit look manly.

She felt a surprising pang of attraction, followed almost immediately by a rather embarrassed flush in her cheeks. Okay, so yes, as her reaction to the firemen at her dorm had proven, she wasn't dead yet. But really? Instant attraction to one of Santa's elves? Seriously?

"I'm so sorry," she muttered to the man's back because that's what you did when you were a mature adult and you bumped into someone because you were too busy paying attention to your cell phone than the people around you.

"No problem," he said as he turned around to face her with a polite grin on his face.

And she found herself staring into the same sparkling, deep blue eyes that still haunted her dreams.

Santa's elf was her ex-boyfriend Rory.

"I'm going to kill my aunt," she muttered.

***

Rory Demeter hated the elf costume. He hated the whole idea of the elf costume, but at least he only had to wear it long enough to film the Crafty Dudes segment of his podcast. Vlog. Whatever.

He still wasn't sure how he wanted to brand his YouTube channel. All he really knew was that he wanted to convince other guys that needlework wasn't just for women. That needlework could be therapeutic and could heal the mind just like the work he did as a physical therapist helped heal the body. Since it was the Christmas season, he figured that if a guy like him (former college football star, however briefly) dressed up in a holiday elf costume, it might attract some attention on social media.

After all, costumes worked well for some of the tabletop gaming guys on YouTube. His roommate used to watch the same roleplaying card game videos over and over again, which might have made Rory sick to death of the game if the guys in the videos hadn't been so entertaining. He'd been shocked at how many subscribers that channel had. He could only hope to have that popular a channel someday.

To do that, he needed to make his podcast more entertaining. The question was how. Watching someone work a cross-stitch was the very definition of boring. If the elf costume didn't attract some attention, he wasn't sure what he should try next.

He was deep in thought, partly looking through the crowded aisles at Stella's Stitchers for the few colors of embroidery thread he still needed for his next cross-stitch project—a clipper ship on the high seas—and partly trying to figure out if he could afford to hire someone (or maybe learn how) to create some snappy animation for his podcasts when he was jolted back to reality by someone running into him from behind.

"I'm so sorry," said a vaguely familiar woman's voice from somewhere in the vicinity of his shoulder blades.

"No problem," he said, curious now about why he recognized the voice.

He turned around and got the shock of his life.

The woman behind him was his ex-high school girlfriend, Kelsey Nichols.

Kelsey. The girl he'd been madly in love with when he was seventeen. The girl he might have married if his family hadn't moved to Hawaii.

The girl he'd thought about trying to look up ever since he'd moved back to Reno six weeks ago. He just hadn't been able to work up the courage. After all, he'd been the one who'd finally decided that he would rather break his own heart (and hers) by ending their relationship than keep on hurting her because they couldn't be together. She probably hated him for that.

And probably still did if the flushed, angry expression on her face was any indication.

"I'm going to kill my aunt," she muttered.

Her aunt? He had no idea what she meant, but he needed to say something. He just wasn't sure what.

"Kel," he managed to get out. "I…uh…"

She gave her head a little shake, then gifted him with a brilliant, if shocked, smile. "Rory," she said, then paused as she didn't know what else to say.

She still had the same gorgeous brown eyes, warm and loving and tipped up just enough at the corners to give herself a playful look. She'd been the prettiest girl in school. Long, thick, curly brown hair, just a smattering of freckles across a pert nose that flushed pink when she was out in the cold, and she fit just right leaning against him when they sat next to each other on his parents' couch and he put his arm around her shoulders.

She hadn't grown any taller over the years—women got their growth spurt early, his dad used to tell him when he'd complained that suddenly all the girls in middle school were taller than he was—but she'd developed a maturity she hadn't had back then. Her voice had grown a little fuller, and while she'd been a little too skinny as a teenager, she seemed to have more of a solid presence. Her hair was shorter, only a little past her shoulders, and she'd managed to tame the curls somehow. If she wore any makeup, it was understated. She certainly didn't need any.

A middle-aged woman excused herself as she pushed past them in the narrow aisle, and Rory realized that he'd been standing there like a log just staring at her like he couldn't get enough of her. His heart gave a little lurch in his chest when he realized that she'd been staring at *him* the same way.

The spell broken, Kelsey glanced down at her feet for a moment before looking up at him again. "What are you doing here?" she asked. "Dressed like..." She gestured at his costume with one hand.

He felt his own cheeks heat up. "Filming a segment for my podcast," he said. "Crafty Dudes. I borrowed the costume." And he had to get it back to his friend Matthew before his shift in the mall as one of Santa's helpers started that afternoon. Which meant he didn't have a whole lot of time left to film the segment for his podcast.

"Crafty dudes," she said, a delightful frown building between her brows.

He shrugged. "I cross stitch," he said, "and I host a podcast to encourage other guys to try the same thing. Stella has a back room she uses to teach people different needle crafts. On Saturdays, I get together with a group of guys back there to work on whatever everyone's working on." He shrugged again, aware that his face was heating up as she kept looking at him like she couldn't decide if he was adorable or nuts. "I film part of it for my podcast."

He glanced toward the back of the store. How come he wasn't embarrassed to share his crafting with anyone else in the world, but he was embarrassed to share it with her?

Because you're afraid she won't respect you, an annoying little voice in his head said. *You're afraid she won't love you anymore.*

"That's why," she said so softly he almost didn't hear her.

Now it was his turn to frown. "Why what?"

She heaved a deep sigh and shook her head, but when she looked at him again, she had the same impish grin on her face that he remembered from their snowball fights—the same grin she had right before she shoved a gloveful of snow in his face.

"I don't know the first thing about cross stitch," she said instead of answering his question. "Why don't you introduce me to the guys, and you can show me what you all do."

***

The old attraction had come back full force and smacked her right in the face as soon as she'd recognized Rory. Damn it. As much as she didn't like the idea of having been set up, she couldn't deny how seeing Rory again after all these year made her feel.

He'd changed. She had too, but damn, he'd become even

better looking, if that was possible. He'd been taller than she'd been back when they were going out, but he looked an inch or two taller now. His shoulders had certainly filled out. She didn't remember him being a wall of muscle, even when he was working out for the football team. His cheekbones were more defined now, and so was his jawline. His hair was the same thick, rich, dark brown, although now he had it cut in a more classic, adult style.

The thing she had trouble reconciling between the Rory she'd known back then and Rory now was that he'd apparently caught part of her aunt's addiction to needlecrafts.

He cross-stitched?

She'd never considered that guys did needlecrafts, but apparently Rory wasn't alone. Three other guys sat around a table in the back room at Stella's, all working with some form of fabric, needles, and yarn or thread.

A small camera was set up on a tabletop tripod at one end of the table and aimed at the other end where a twenty-something guy sat knitting.

"Captain Picard knits," he said when Rory introduced her.

She shot Rory a confused look.

"Patrick Stewart," Rory said, "the actor."

Ah. That must have been one of his roles. Kelsey didn't watch a lot of television. Grad students who also worked as graduate assistants had no time for television. She'd rather bury her nose in a good book during what little free time she had.

"A lot of guys knit," Rory said as he futzed with the camera. Apparently satisfied, he took the empty seat next to the guy who was knitting something in Christmas colors. "Ready guys?" he asked.

They all nodded, and then Rory shot the camera a brilliant smile. "Welcome to the holiday segment of Crafty Guys!" he said.

Kelsey's heart melted all over again, just like it had when she was sixteen.

She sat at the far end of the table and watched as Rory recorded his segment. He was a natural with the camera and with the guys in the group. He got them talking about their projects, which were all holiday related. The guy whose role model was apparently Patrick Stewart was knitting a holiday sweater for his baby niece. Another guy, this one in his sixties, was crocheting little animals for his grandkids for Christmas.

"Crocheting helps keep the arthritis at bay," he said to the camera. "And the kids are little enough they like the toys. Give them another couple of years, and they'll be too cool to want things like this from Grandpa."

"My niece won't," said the guy knitting the baby sweater.

Rory had some sort of remote gadget attached to the tripod so that the camera swiveled just enough from side to side to follow the conversation from speaker to speaker. He made sure each guy in the group got time on camera, including a guy in his forties in a red plaid shirt who didn't talk a lot. He was working on a cross-stitch ornament for his daughter. "She lives with her mom," was all he'd say about his family.

There was a story there, Kelsey was sure of it, and it would probably break her heart if he told it. If she'd been a journalism major, she might have tried to pry it out of him, but she wasn't. The communications she was interested in were the kind that happened naturally—or that a savvy company could make appear to happen naturally.

Rory had a gift for communication. He'd probably always

had it, but she'd been too busy noticing his other qualities back when they'd been in high school. She certainly had an opportunity now. She sat forward in her chair, arms leaning on the table, and watched, fascinated, as Rory worked the small group until he turned off the camera and she realized that nearly an hour had gone by.

All the guys packed up their projects. Some cleared their throat behind Kelsey, and when she turned her head, she saw her aunt standing in the open door to the back room. Addy had a bemused grin on her face.

"Should I come back later?" Addy asked.

Rory stopped what he was doing and looked at Kelsey. "I have to get this costume back, but I was wondering if you had time for coffee first." He glanced at Addy, but he didn't seem to recognize her. "Unless you have plans."

Had Rory ever met her aunt? Kelsey couldn't remember. Maybe this wasn't a setup after all, but it couldn't be a total coincidence.

"Rory," she said, "this is my Aunt Adeline."

"Addy," her aunt said, coming into the room and holding out her hand to Rory, which he shook. "I hear the coffee shop across the way is superb," she added, her eyes twinkling. "I imagine the two of you have a lot to catch up on."

Oh, yes. This was definitely a setup, if only on her aunt's part.

"I have a little more shopping to do," Addy said as she patted Kelsey on the shoulder on her way out of the back room. "Call me when you're ready."

You can bet on it, Kelsey thought. *Rory and I aren't the only ones who have a lot to talk about.*

***

255

The drive-thru coffee stand also had a walkup window and a couple of wrought-iron tables and chairs by the walkup window to accommodate customers not in cars. It wasn't the best spot for an impromptu date with the woman you'd only recently discovered you were still in love with, but the day was warm enough for November and sunny, and Kelsey was smiling at him in the kind of way that he almost—*almost*— didn't mind that he was still dressed in a Santa's elf costume.

"How did you get started cross-stitching?" she asked.

She was leaning forward in her seat, her arms on the table just like she'd been sitting in the back room at Stella's, only now she had her hands wrapped around her latte. She looked warm enough in her puffy jacket and jeans, but he still had a desire to wrap his arm around her shoulders and hold her tight just to make sure.

"Rehab," he said, taking a sip of coffee.

One of her eyebrows rose, and a shadow clouded her warm, brown eyes.

"Oh, not that kind," he added, realizing that like most people, she probably thought of rehab as something to do with addiction. "I blew out my knee, junior year."

That was an understatement. It had taken three surgeries and months and months of rehab to repair the damage a three-hundred-pound defensive lineman had done to Rory's left leg. A career-ending injury, his coach and doctors had agreed.

"Spent a lot of time sitting on my ass feeling sorry for myself," he said, not looking at her. "One of my physical therapists suggested I take up crocheting."

"Like the guy who's making toys for his grandkids?" she asked.

He snorted. "Nothing as involved as that. I made afghans."

"Afghans."

"Yeah, my mom still has them."

He realized he'd clenched his hands around his own paper coffee container. She reached across the table and touched the back of his hand.

Just that simple touched warmed him in a way he hadn't felt in a long, long time. He took her hand in his, and she smiled at him.

"Anyway," he said, "crochet didn't do it for me. Even though it took my mind off the pain, it got old after a while. So my therapist suggested cross-stitch. Following the pattern, seeing how it all comes together—that kept my mind engaged. Gave me something to look forward to." He shrugged. "Gave me my major."

"What's that?"

"Sports therapy," he said. "That's why I came back here, to work with the therapists up at the university."

One of the reasons, if he was being honest with himself. He could have stayed in Hawaii, where his parents still lived, and worked with the university there, but Hawaii had never really felt like home.

"I bet you're great at it," she said, giving his hand a squeeze. "I saw how you connected with the guys in there. You're a natural."

Not that it seemed to help his podcast much.

They sat holding hands and talking—catching up, as her aunt had put it—until they'd both finished their drinks. She told him about her graduate work and career plans, and the fire at her dorm which made her come home earlier than she'd planned.

"How long are you staying?" he asked.

"Not sure," she said, glancing away. "Probably until the dorm's ready to move back into."

He took a slow breath to steady his nerves. Now came the tricky part. Sure, they seemed to connect almost like no time had passed, but was she just being polite? Just being friends? Or did she want something more?

"So," he said, drawing the word out. "You want to catch dinner and a movie while you're here?"

"Catch dinner?"

"I meant *go out* for dinner and *catch* a movie," he said, embarrassed, but then he realized she was giving him one of her impish grins.

"How about tomorrow?" she asked. "Are you free?"

Even if he wasn't before, he was now. He wasn't seventeen anymore. He'd go to the moon and back for this woman.

"You've got yourself a date."

***

What in the world had she just done?

Agreed to a date with her old boyfriend, that's what. Just how stupid could she be?

He probably had all sorts of women after him. Just look at him! He was gorgeous and charming and he'd been a star quarterback in college!

She had no reason to believe that just because she'd decided not to get seriously involved with anyone after they'd broken up that he hadn't "dated" a series of beautiful women. And here she'd just volunteered to be yet another woman in what was probably a long, long line.

And all because her old feelings had reared their ugly head thanks to an encounter that wasn't as chance as it had first appeared.

Well, she'd just have to call him and cancel their date, that's all. She'd spent too many years protecting her poor heart to have it broken all over again.

"You're certainly quiet," Addy said after they got back to her aunt's little A-frame house. "I expected you to read me the riot act."

They were sitting in the living room, Addy in her craft chair—an overstuffed recliner positioned to the side of a gas fireplace in just the perfect spot for the natural light that came through the front window when the curtains were open—and Kelsey in a wingback chair on the other side of the fireplace. Addy was working on her needlecraft pillowtop with the new yarn she'd bought at Stella's. Kelsey had a book propped open on her lap, but she'd only been pretending to read. She couldn't stop thinking about Rory and how good it had felt holding hands with him. How warm it had made her feel—warm and protected, just like when she used to snuggle against him on his parents' couch while they watched TV.

"Didn't your coffee date with Rory go well?" Addy asked.

Kelsey closed her book. "It went too well."

Addy nodded. "And that's the problem, isn't it." She put her needlework aside and stood up. "Stay here," she said. "I want to show you something."

Addy left the living room, and a minute later Kelsey heard her aunt pulling down the fold-up ladder that led up to the A-frame's attic. Addy used to have her office up there before she'd sold her accounting business and retired. Kelsey had only been up there a few times when she'd been younger and visited with her parents. The room was oddly triangle shaped, with the walls on both sides also serving as the ceiling, and round windows on both ends. Addy and her parents could only stand up straight in the very center.

Apparently Addy used the attic for storage these days because a few moments later she came back with a dusty wooden box only a little larger than a shoebox. She sat back down in her overstuffed recliner and opened the box. She shuffled through the papers inside, then pulled out an envelope the size of a birthday card. The envelope had yellowed around the edges and appeared stuffed with photographs.

Addy took out one of the photographs and leaned forward to hold it out to Kelsey.

"My husband," Addy said with a wistful smile. "Justin."

What? As far as Kelsey knew, Addy had never been married. Her dad used to refer to Addy as Kelsey's maiden aunt, and she had the same last name as Kelsey's mother's maiden name.

The man in the photograph had scruffy dark hair longer than Kelsey's. He was thin, almost skinny, and wore a colorful patterned shirt and pants with a wide white belt. He had long sideburns and wore glasses with round lenses. In the picture he had his arm around a woman who was clearly a much, much younger version of Addy.

"I'm not sure how much your mother told you about our childhood," Addy said, "but between the two of us, I was the older, more rebellious sister. When your mother was mother was eleven and I was seventeen, I ran away from home. To be with Justin."

Kelsey stared at the photo, then stared at her aunt, trying to reconcile the two versions of the woman she'd known all her life.

"We'd met at a friend's house," Addy said. "We hit it off

almost immediately—like you and Rory, from what your mother told me."

Addy handed Kelsey another picture. In this one, Justin and Addy were sitting next to each other on a blanket in someone's backyard, surrounded by other kids their age. Justin had on shorts, no shirt, and Addy was wearing swimsuit. The photo was yellowed around the edges, just like the envelope it had been kept in.

"He was only in town for the summer, but we fell hard for each other." Addy gazed down at the box in her lap. "When he went back home, we wrote letters to each other. I still have every one."

Kelsey didn't doubt it. She'd never heard her aunt talk with such deep emotion in her voice. Her eyes were shiny bright as she gazed down at the box, but her cheeks were dry.

"We planned to get married after we both turned eighteen, but we couldn't wait. So when he turned eighteen, I ran away to be with him. He helped me get a fake I.D.—very scandalous —and we got married on a beach in California."

She handed Kelsey one more photograph, this one of Addy and Justin standing on a beach, the sun setting on the far horizon and glittering off the ocean waves.

"Just the two of us, with a couple of surfers for witnesses and one of his friends to officiate the wedding."

No one in Kelsey's family had ever spoken of this. "What happened?" she asked, already knowing what had to be the answer.

"Justin was a surfer, you see," Addy said. "That's why we were married on the beach. We lived in a house by the ocean with a bunch of other people—very, *very* scandalous."

Kelsey only had a few memories of her grandparents on

her mother's side. They'd been much older than her dad's parents, although all her grandparents were gone now. But what she did remember was that her mom's parents had been very strict and conservative and disapproving of anything that might embarrass them in public. She could just imagine their reaction to the man Addy had fallen in love with.

"Six months after we were married, Justin went out surfing and didn't come back," Addy said.

Addy might not be crying, but tears sprang to Kelsey's eyes. Addy had said that so matter of factly, like it was just another part of life.

"I came back home," Addy said, "because I couldn't stand the sight of the ocean. I still can't, that's why I live among the trees."

She held out her hand, and Kelsey handed her the photographs. Addy put them back in the envelope and returned the envelope to the box.

"My parents had the marriage annulled," Addy said. "Not that I'd taken Justin's last name. I was very independent that way." She gave Kelsey a quick smile. "I packed up my memories and my heart, put it all in this box, and told myself I'd never find another love like that in my life. I didn't want my heart broken like that again, you see."

She closed the box and stood up suddenly, wiping one hand across her face.

"Oh, my," she said. "I haven't looked in this box in years, although I will tell you that I think of Justin every day, and I say goodnight to him every night before I go to sleep."

Kelsey stared at the gas fireplace, at the dancing flames, but she didn't really see it. Instead she was imagining what life would be like if she'd never seen Rory again.

"I need to go put this back," Abby said. "I didn't mean for this to become maudlin, because that's not how I feel. I've had a good long life, and I'm happy with my life. Happy with my choice not to look for love again." She squeezed Kelsey's shoulder. "I just wanted to let you know that I understood your decision to be on your own, and if you decide to stay on your own, I'll understand that too. You're both different people now and that gives you a lot to think about. Just…"

Kelsey looked up at her aunt. "Don't blow it?" she said.

Addy nodded. "I believe that's the appropriate phrase." She cocked her head to one side. "Although come to think of it, if you're letting your head get in the way of your heart, I think your heart just answered all of your fears."

"What do you mean?"

Addy squeezed her shoulder again, then let go. "Your head's telling you all these reasons why it won't work with Rory, why you shouldn't take a chance on getting hurt again, right?"

"Pretty much." That's all she'd been doing ever since Addy had picked her up and the glow of her coffee date with Rory had worn off.

"Well," Addy said, "your heart just told you 'don't blow it.' So what are you waiting for? Follow your heart."

***

Kelsey wasn't only the most gorgeous, most wonderful woman in the world, she was also the smartest.

In the two weeks since they'd been dating, she'd not only completely reignited the passion he'd felt for her back when he'd been seventeen, she'd revamped his passion for the podcast he'd been working on for what seemed like forever.

It turned out that she could actually do the animation he'd

wanted to do use to spiff up his podcasts. "Digital media minor," she'd said. "I learned how to do all sorts of media stuff."

She helped him cut the Crafty Dudes segment of his Christmas podcast to get rid of all the clunky shifts from his rotating camera. She researched other websites that targeted men who stitched, and even found a video of a guy on stage discussing the type of cross-stitching that would appeal to men.

"You could do that," she'd told him. "You're certainly charismatic enough." She'd kissed him lightly on the lips, which they'd been doing ever since he'd dropped her off after their second movie date. "You could convince guys about the therapeutic benefits of cross-stitching and crochet. If Patrick Stewart can knit, real men can stitch."

In fact, thanks to her suggestion, he'd renamed his podcast from Crafty Dudes to Real Men Can Stitch. She helped him set up a mailing list, a Facebook group, and worked on his website to set up behind the scenes things he didn't understand.

In just one week, the subscribers to his YouTube channel jumped from twenty-eight to fifty-seven. It wasn't huge, but it was a start.

The only thing she hadn't done was ask him to teach her how to cross-stitch. "It's your thing," she said.

Well, in truth, that wasn't the only thing she hadn't done. So far, they hadn't gone beyond holding hands and kissing each other lightly, although for his part he certainly felt strong enough to take things further. But this was Kelsey. They'd broken each other's hearts before, and he understood if she wanted to take it slow. He'd give her all the time in the world so long as he could keep feeling this happy. Even the guys he worked with at the university had started to tease him about being in love.

Things were going so perfectly, he was almost afraid that something would happen to spoil it.

Two days before Christmas, something finally did.

"The dorm's ready," she said when he came to pick her up at her aunt's house for their dinner date.

A light snow had begun to fall that afternoon. The snow looked so pretty falling among the pines, just enough of the white stuff to dust the driveway up to her aunt's house and turn the tip of Kelsey's nose an adorable shade of pink.

She was sitting in the passenger seat of his SUV, wrapped up in her puffy jacket, the silver charm he'd given her the previous weekend as an early Christmas present hanging from a thin silver chain around her neck. Her eyes were darker than normal, filled with emotion. The SUV's heater had warmed up the car nicely, but her words had chilled him to the bone, especially since he knew what had to be coming next.

"I'm going home," she said.

***

Kelsey couldn't remember the last time she'd been so nervous.

Tisha had texted her earlier in the day to tell her that the dorm was ready. *Don't know if you've checked your email, girlfriend*, the text had read, *but we can move back whenever we want. After a month with the 'rents, I'm soooo ready!*

Kelsey had planned to spend at least two weeks working on her graduate assignments, but she'd been so busy with Rory, she hadn't even opened her laptop except to work on his website and his podcast. She told herself that was real-world work experience, the kind she hoped to do for clients one day, but that hadn't really been it.

She'd done it to see the look on Rory's face when his ideas came to life.

She still couldn't believe how wonderful it made her feel. Lighter than air. Lighter than all the days she'd spent dreaming about how fulfilling that kind of work might be, and the nights she'd spent dreaming about him. Wondering what he was doing in his life, and if he ever thought about her.

Well, she knew what he thought about her now. He loved her, plain and simple. He hadn't come right out and said it—neither had she—but she knew. All those stupid worries she'd had right after their first coffee date, she'd put those to rest. They had just been stupid worries. Her heart had been right. Addy had been right. Rory loved her and she loved him, and they weren't teenagers anymore.

The fact that she had to go back to school didn't have to mean the end of their relationship. Did it? But she had to go. She was too far behind in her classes to stay, and she'd worked too hard toward her degree to stop now.

He had to understand. He just had to. He'd worked hard for where he was, too.

She sat in his SUV in her aunt's driveway, snow falling softly around them. The way snow muffled everything, she felt like they were the only two people in the world, and nothing the world could do would hurt them.

The light from the dashboard made his blue eyes look deeper than ever. "When?" he asked. His voice sounded strained.

She licked her suddenly dry lips. "The 27th." She'd bought the bus ticket that afternoon so she wouldn't change her mind.

"I won't leave before Christmas." They'd already made plans for the day that included Addy, a Christmas ham, hot chocolate, and lots of old holiday movies.

He smiled at her, but his smile seemed as strained as his voice. "Then I guess we'll make the most of the next few days, right?"

He went to put the SUV in gear, but she put her hand on his to stop him.

"Before we go," she said, "I have an early present for you." She took a little box from the pocket of her jacket and gave it to him. Addy had helped her tie the bow.

Her heart hammered in her chest as he unwrapped the present. He fumbled with the wrapping paper, then made a joke out of ripping it off with an exaggerated grunt.

When he unwrapped the little cross-stitch ornament inside, his mouth fell open. "You made this?" he asked, his voice full of wonder.

It wasn't much, just a sprig of mistletoe stitched in green floss on white cloth. The cross-stitched bow on top of the mistletoe was a single shade of red, which thankfully didn't show the tiny spots from when she'd pricked her fingertips with the end of the blunt needle she'd learned how to use to make the pattern. Good thing that needle hadn't been as sharp as the needle Addy had used to sew the cross-stitched part onto the backing that turned the whole thing into an ornament, complete with hanger, or he would have noticed all the bandages on her fingers.

"Addy helped," she said. "I wanted to keep it a secret."

He didn't say anything, just sat staring at it so long her nerves nearly jangled her out of her seat.

"Do you like it?" she finally asked.

"Like it?" He held it up to the light from the dashboard. "You even put your initials on it."

"Addy said I should, that that's what cross-stitchers do."

He closed his hand around it and held it against his chest. "I love it," he said. Then with his other hand, he took her chin gently and leaned toward her, bringing their faces together. "I love you."

Before she could respond, he kissed her. Not the gentle kisses they'd had so far, but a deeper, more thorough kiss. The kind she remembered from their teenage years. The kind where when the kiss ended, she wasn't sitting next to him anymore, but he'd leaned over her and was holding her like she was the most precious thing in the world.

When the kiss ended, she realized he was now holding the mistletoe ornament over their heads. "I believe it's tradition," he said with the kind of smile that melted all her nerves away.

"I love you too," she said. "We'll work it out this time, right? It's only a two-hour bus ride away. Much closer than Hawaii."

He kissed her again. "Much closer. Much less water."

Another kiss.

"Much less," she agreed.

She didn't know how long they sat there, kissing and telling each other how much they loved each other, and making plans for visits and who would travel where. They steamed up the inside of the SUV's windows as the snow continued to fall. They only broke apart when Kelsey heard a rapping on the driver's side window.

Rory rolled his window down just enough for her to see Addy standing in the snow, a scarf thrown over her head.

Kelsey smiled at her aunt, a ridiculously happy grin.

"I came out to see if everything was okay," Addy said, "but I can clearly see that it is. I'd suggest you get a room, though. I don't have many neighbors out here, but the ones I do might complain. Unless you want to come inside. I can listen to a book. I do have noise-cancelling headphone somewhere."

Even in the light from the dash, Kelsey could see that Rory was blushing up to his hairline.

"Uh, that's okay," he managed to stammer out. "I think we'll just go get that dinner now."

Addy gave them a little finger wave goodbye, and Rory rolled up the window.

"That's right, right?" he asked. "Dinner?"

"Dinner," she agreed.

Dinner first. Afterwards? They had all the time in the world for afterwards.

He loved her, and she knew she loved him. They'd been given a second chance, and she intended to take it and run with it for all it was worth.

Everything else was just details. They weren't kids anymore, and the details would take care of themselves.

NEWSLETTER SIGN-UP

DEAN WESLEY SMITH

Sign up for the Dean Wesley Smith newsletter, and keep up with the latest news, releases and so much more—even the occasional giveaway.

Go to **deanwesleysmith.com.**

Sign up for the WMG Publishing newsletter, too, and get the latest news and releases from all of the WMG authors and lines, including *Pulphouse Fiction Magazine, Smith's Monthly,* and so much more.

To sign up go to **wmgpublishing.com.**

Follow Dean on BookBub

ABOUT THE EDITOR

DEAN WESLEY SMITH

Considered one of the most prolific writers working in modern fiction, with more than 30 million books sold, *USA Today* bestselling writer Dean Wesley Smith published far more than a hundred novels in forty years, and hundreds of short stories across many genres.

At the moment he produces novels in several major series, including the time travel Thunder Mountain novels set in the Old West, the galaxy-spanning Seeders Universe series, the urban fantasy Ghost of a Chance series, a superhero series starring Poker Boy, and a mystery series featuring the retired detectives of the Cold Poker Gang.

His monthly magazine, *Smith's Monthly*, which consists of only his own fiction, premiered in October 2013 and offers readers more than 70,000 words per issue, including a new and original novel every month.

During his career, Dean also wrote a couple dozen *Star Trek* novels, the only two original *Men in Black* novels, Spider-Man and X-Men novels, plus novels set in gaming and television worlds. Writing with his wife Kristine Kathryn Rusch under the name Kathryn Wesley, he wrote the novel for the NBC miniseries The Tenth Kingdom and other books for *Hallmark Hall of Fame* movies.

He wrote novels under dozens of pen names in the worlds

of comic books and movies, including novelizations of almost a dozen films, from *The Final Fantasy* to *Steel* to *Rundown*.

Dean also worked as a fiction editor off and on, starting at Pulphouse Publishing, then at *VB Tech Journal*, then Pocket Books, and now at WMG Publishing, where he and Kristine Kathryn Rusch serve as series editors for the acclaimed *Fiction River* anthology series.

For more information about Dean's books and ongoing projects, please visit his website at www.deanwesley-smith.com and sign up for his newsletter.

For more information:
www.deanwesleysmith.com

f facebook.com/deanwsmith3
p patreon.com/deanwesleysmith
BB bookbub.com/authors/dean-wesley-smith

www.ingramcontent.com/pod-product-compliance
Lightning Source LLC
Chambersburg PA
CBHW010729100726
47899CB00009B/2984

* 9 7 8 1 5 6 1 4 6 9 9 9 4 *